A strange, knowing look came to Diana's eyes.

"Something tells me you're going to hear something from Polimar very, very soon," she said.

Pres chuckled. "You been hanging out with Darcy Laken and getting those psychic flashes?"

"Hang out with that freak?" Diana spat. "Are you kidding?"

"It is amazing what spews out of your mouth, do you know that?" Emma asked in a low voice.

"So, Diana," Sly asked, ignoring Emma's remark, "what makes you so sure we're gonna hear from the label?"

Diana got a beatific smile on her face. "I don't know," she said lightly. "I might not hang out with Darcy, but maybe I am just a little, teeny bit psychic, myself."

The SUNSET ISLAND series
by Cherie Bennett

Also created by Cherie Bennett

Sunset Revenge

CHERIE BENNETT

Sunset™ Island

SPLASH™

A BERKLEY / SPLASH BOOK

SUNSET REVENGE is an original publication of The Berkley Publishing Group. This work has never appeared before in book form.

SUNSET REVENGE

A Berkley Book / published by arrangement with General Licensing Company, Inc.

PRINTING HISTORY
Berkley edition / May 1994

All rights reserved.
Copyright © 1994 by General Licensing Company, Inc.
Cover art copyright © 1994 by
General Licensing Company, Inc.
This book may not be reproduced in whole or in part, by mimeograph or any other means, without permission.
For information address: General Licensing Company, Inc., 24 West 25th Street, New York, New York 10010.

A GLC BOOK

Splash and *Sunset Island* are trademarks belonging to General Licensing Company, Inc.

ISBN: 0-425-14228-0

BERKLEY®
Berkley Books are published by
The Berkley Publishing Group,
200 Madison Avenue, New York, New York 10016.
BERKLEY and the "B" design
are trademarks belonging to Berkley Publishing Corporation.

PRINTED IN THE UNITED STATES OF AMERICA

10 9 8 7 6 5 4 3 2 1

For my darling

ONE

"I really can't believe it," Kristy Powell said smugly, sliding into a chair at the booth at the Play Café. "All four of you girls sitting around the same table. And no one is even chucking a drink at anyone else!"

"Yet," Samantha—Sam—Bridges pointed out sweetly, giving Kristy her most winning smile.

Kristy shook her shoulder-length blond hair back over her shoulders. "Well, I'm disappointed," she admitted, taking out her tape recorder and setting it up on the table. "When my editor for the *Breakers* told me to do an article about the girls of New England's hottest up-and-coming rock band, Flirting With Danger, I figured the only possible angle of interest would have to be that nasty rumor that you all can't stand each other!"

"Actually, we all love each other," Sam said, pushing some of her long, wild, red hair back off her face. "It's just Diana we can't stand."

Kristy clicked on the tape recorder and leaned toward Sam eagerly. "Care to make that statement for the record?"

"Jealousy is such a petty little emotion," Diana De Witt sighed before Sam could reply. She turned to Kristy. "But then Sam can't help being a petty little person. Can you, Sam?"

Sam opened her mouth to zing one back at Diana, but just then Emma Cresswell, one of Sam's two best friends in the world and the third backup singer for the Flirts, kicked her under the table.

"We should talk about the band, I think," Emma suggested in her soft, well-bred voice, deftly turning the interview in a safer direction.

"But this is so much more interesting," Kristy exclaimed, a wicked grin on her face. She cocked her head to one side. "Now, why is it that you all loathe and detest each other so much?"

"Hey, how about some pictures?" Carrie Alden cried, springing out of her seat. She was Sam's other best friend, and she was at this meeting to take photos for the newspaper article. And at the moment, she was trying hard to protect Sam from her own big mouth. When Carrie had heard from Emma and Sam that Kristy was going to be doing the interview, she'd called the *Breakers* photo editor and begged him to let her take the pictures for the piece. To Carrie's surprise, the editor had said yes.

"Snap away," Kristy told Carrie, as the waitress laid an extra-large cheese pizza on the table. "Candid shots are the best," she added, helping herself to a slice of the pizza. Everyone else took a piece, except Sam, who took two.

Carrie pointed the camera at the girls, snapping off shots from different angles as they ate.

The girls were all wearing their official Flirting With Danger tour jackets over plain white T-shirts, but they looked so different from one another that no one would have any question as to who was who: Sam, with her lanky five feet, ten-inch frame, wild red hair, and trademark red cowboy boots; Emma, with her naturally blond straight hair, which framed her heart-shaped face and enhanced her patrician good looks; and Diana, with curly chestnut hair, piercing blue eyes, and a perfectly aerobicized body that looked like an advertisement for a fitness center. Carrie was wearing her official Flirting With Danger tour jacket, too (she'd briefly been in the band when Diana had been injured on tour), and she looked girl-next-door cute in her own unaffected way. She snapped off a last shot of Sam, who was licking a string of melted cheese off her pinky, and then she sat back down and put her camera carefully next to her on the floor.

"So," Kristy said, as she polished off her slice of pizza, "I want to hear about the Three Musketeers. I mean you—Sam and Emma— and Madam Photographer, here."

"Uh, excuse me," Diana interrupted coldly, "but just because Carrie is a groupie for the band's lead singer doesn't mean she's actually in the band."

"Groupie?" Carrie repeated, seething. "Billy is my boyfriend—"

"Whatever," Diana said airily. She turned to Kristy. "She's still not in the band."

"I know," Kristy replied, then she turned

back to the other three girls. Diana made a disgusted noise under her breath and folded her arms angrily. Kristy ignored her. "You all were friends before you joined the band. How'd you guys hook up? Emma?"

"In a funny way, really," Emma said slowly. "It was the oddest thing. We all met at the International Au Pair Convention in New York City the spring before last. I was really nervous, I remember—"

"Me, too," Carrie agreed, smiling at Emma.

"It was going to be my very first job—if I even got hired, that is," Emma recalled. She grinned at Sam and Carrie. "And, well, the three of us just . . . hit it off!"

"We all picked Sunset Island as our first choice," Carrie added. "And luckily, we all got jobs here."

"This is our second summer," Emma continued. "All three of us decided to come back after our first year of college. . . ."

"Not me. I dropped out to become a professional dancer," Sam interrupted blithely, polishing off her second slice of pizza.

"Well, anyway," Emma continued, "we all came back here and . . . I guess that's it!"

"What she didn't mention," Sam added,

reaching for another slice of pizza, "is how different we are. I mean, I'm from Junction, Kansas—which is so small it barely exists—Carrie is from the 'burbs of New Jersey, and Emma is your basic hotsy-totsy Boston heiress—"

"Sam!" Emma exclaimed, reddening. She hated being singled out for her money, particularly in a newspaper article.

"And another thing," Sam continued obliviously, "Carrie over there is, like, a major brain and a killer photographer—I mean, the girl goes to Yale. And Emma is more than your basic perfect face—she's planning to join the Peace Corps. And as for *moi*, I will soon be starring in *Lifestyles of the Rich and Famous*." Sam reached for her glass of Coke and guzzled it down.

"Only if you sleep with someone rich and famous," Diana put in.

"You ought to know," Sam snapped back, "since you sleep with everyone."

"Oh, witty comeback," Diana said sarcastically. She turned to Kristy. "Look, I have things to do. I thought this was supposed to be a *band* interview."

"It is," Kristy assured her. "I understand

6

that you knew at least one of the others before the band began."

"That's right," Diana agreed coolly. "I know Emma from when we were both in boarding school together. In Europe. Very rich, very exclusive, very boring," she added.

Emma winced. Try as she could to overcome it, she was still having a hard time dealing with being treated only as the daughter of Brent and Kat Cresswell and sole heiress to the Cresswell multi-millions.

Kristy nodded. "So, you're all au pairs here on the island now?"

"Please," Diana uttered. "They are, I'm not. Do I look like the babysitter type?"

Sam wanted to smack her. *I hate that bitch so much. We're a lot more than babysitters! We basically help run our bosses' households. Diana ought to try it—she'll see what real work is like for a change.*

"So, the band is full-time for you?" Kristy asked Diana.

Diana nodded, and played with the diamond stud in her left ear. "That and songwriting," she said.

"With who?" Kristy asked.

"Mostly Pres," Diana answered, a malicious gleam in her eye. She gave Sam an evil grin. "He really, really inspires me, if you know what I mean."

Sam's hands clenched into fists under the table. For the better part of a summer and a half, she and Presley Travis, the bass player for the Flirts, had been an on-again-off-again item—mostly on. But earlier in the summer, she and Pres had split, apparently for good, because Pres had gotten tired of Sam's flirting with other guys. By the time Sam realized Pres was the one she really wanted, it was too late.

It still hurts, Sam thought bleakly. *But lately Pres has seemed warmer to me, and we did kiss on the beach recently, so maybe there's hope, and—*

"Pres and I are very, very close," Diana added in a low, sexy voice. "Feel free to quote me." She gave Sam another smug look of triumph.

Sam felt Emma kick her under the table again. *I know what that kick means,* Sam realized. *It means that Diana is just trying to get to me. She's probably lying through her teeth. I hope.*

"Everyone in the band is close," Emma said

8

smoothly. "We've been on tour together, and, well, we really care about one another."

"Now, isn't *that* boring copy," Diana told Kristy. She leaned confidentially toward the reporter. "But that's nothing," she whispered. "The real story is about Emma's wedding. Why don't you ask about that?"

"Why don't you let Kristy do her own interview?" Emma snapped.

"A sensitive subject?" Diana asked innocently.

"Actually, I was just coming to that," Kristy asked.

"What does my personal life have to do with the band?" Emma asked, clearly uncomfortable.

"Not much," Kristy admitted with a shrug. "But I thought I'd ask."

"I'm not answering," Emma said coldly.

"But Emma—" Kristy began.

"I said, I am not answering," Emma repeated, her icy tones sounding exactly like her mother's.

"You've got that privilege," Kristy responded, "and that's what I'll report you said."

"You do that," Emma said coldly.

This time it was Sam's turn to kick Emma under the table. *Wow,* Sam thought. *Emma still can't talk about what happened with Kurt. Well, I don't blame her.*

"So, if you're not going to give me any really good dirt," Kristy said with a grin, "let's get back to the Flirts." She drained the last of her Coke. "I understand there's a good chance that the Flirts will be signing a recording contract."

"Sheldon 'Call-Me-Shelly' Plotkin loves us," Sam replied, as if that explained everything.

"He's A&R for Polimar Records," Diana translated. "Artist and Repertory. If he says we're signing, we're signing."

"It's not that simple," Kristy countered. "I know about the music biz." The tape clicked and she quickly turned it over and pressed the "on" button.

"Well, he did come to New York to hear the band when we were out on tour," Emma pointed out. "He said he's really interested in us."

"You guys got a contract yet?" Kristy asked.

No one said anything. The answer was obviously no.

"I rest my case," Kristy concluded with a shrug. "Don't believe the hype."

"A deal's coming," Diana said finally. "I can feel it."

"Absolutely," Sam agreed firmly.

"I think so," Emma added, nodding.

"Hey, the three of you are agreeing about something!" Kristy said with a laugh.

"And you even got it on tape," Sam pointed out. She sat up a little straighter. "In my opinion, the band is more important than personal squabbles."

"Someone get me a barf bag," Diana groaned.

"So you can wear it on your head?" Sam asked.

"God, I would if it meant I wouldn't have to be seen with you!" Diana exclaimed. "I mean, you shovel the bull so deep it's no wonder the roots of your hair are brown!"

"My hair is naturally red and you know it!" Sam cried. "That is just *so* bitchy—"

"Uh, kiddies," Kristy called to them. Everyone turned to her. "One last question."

"I am a natural redhead," Sam said loudly, leaning in to the tape recorder.

"What you are is a natural *air*-head," Diana corrected.

"This is great, get a photo!" Kristy told Carrie.

Carrie rolled her eyes and snapped away, making sure she only got Diana in the frame so as to not make Sam look bad.

"Here's my last question," Kristy said, "although the answer seems obvious. Isn't it a little hard to sing together up on stage when you obviously hate each other so much?"

"We don't hate each other," Emma said smoothly.

"Yeah, right," Kristy said with a laugh. "You're the best of friends."

"We're professionals," Sam replied with as much dignity as she could muster.

Kristy smiled. "You know, I wasn't that thrilled when my editor assigned me this piece. But now I'm thinking I wouldn't have missed it for the world!" She laughed out loud. "Not for the world!"

Sam got a terrible sinking feeling, and she snuck a look at Emma. Emma didn't look any happier.

Somehow I feel like a log that's about to get a first-class hatchet job, Sam thought miserably. *And I am one log who has a really, really big mouth.*

"My hate for her is boundless," Sam said to Emma, as the two of them lounged together in the backyard of Dan Jacobs's house, where Sam worked. It was the afternoon after the day of interview, and Sam was supposed to be keeping an eye on the two Jacobs twins, Becky and Allie. The twins were fourteen years old, boy crazy, and as far as Sam was concerned, a general pain in the butt.

"Hey, Becky, is that a cigarette?" Sam called to one of the twins, sitting up in her lounge chair.

"No, it's a teeny-tiny telescope," Becky replied. "We're stargazing."

"Yeah, well, if I see you light that teeny-tiny telescope, I'm going to tell your father, who will have a teeny-tiny fit," Sam called to her.

"Fine," Becky snapped, and threw the cigarette back into her purse. She lay down on her large towel and closed her eyes.

"Two o'clock, time to turn over," Allie said, and both twins turned onto their backs. They were wearing matching yellow bikinis with the tops untied so they wouldn't get tan lines. Allie turned the radio up higher until the rock and roll blared across the backyard.

"I don't suppose they use sunscreen," Emma said over the music, looking at the twins.

"All they use is baby oil," Sam said, reaching for the iced tea near her lounge chair. "Forget trying to tell them anything—they know it all."

"Oh, I did, too, when I was fourteen," Emma said. She closed her eyes and turned her face—which was sunscreened—up toward the sun. "Mmmm, this feels great."

"The greatest," Sam agreed, closing her eyes, too.

The two of them were silent for some time.

"I did something weird this morning," Emma said finally, quietly.

"Girlfriend," Sam said broadly, "everything you do is weird." She winked at Emma to let her know that she was kidding.

"No," Emma replied quietly, "I'm serious."

"So? Tell 'Dear Sam,' queen of advice to the lovelorn!"

Emma looked down at the grass. "I . . . I

14

dialed Kurt's number this morning," Emma mumbled.

"But he's in Michigan," Sam answered quickly. "I thought he went there right after—"

Emma nodded. "He did."

"So . . ."

"So I called the number here, anyway," Emma admitted. "I know it's crazy. I know he's in Michigan—I don't even really want to talk to him—but when I passed the telephone in the Hewitts' living room I couldn't help myself!"

Sam looked closely at her friend. *The truth of the matter is, sometimes I think I'm the worst person in the world to give advice about love and guys,* she thought to herself, *but I've got to say something. The question is what?*

"So . . . do you want to talk about it?" Sam asked hesitantly. "I mean, we haven't talked about it much. . . ."

"I don't know," Emma responded, picking up a blade of grass and rubbing it between her fingers. "I honestly don't know."

"Well," Sam said, "I'm not going to push you. When you're ready, I'll listen."

"Thanks," Emma replied, a small smile

15

crossing her face. "You sound as mature as Carrie."

"Yeah, well, I put my foot in my mouth enough at that stupid interview with Kristy yesterday to last me for a few years," Sam admitted. She leaned toward Emma on one elbow. "Just promise me one thing."

"What's that?"

"Promise first!" Sam said, wiggling her eyebrows at Emma.

Emma held up her fingers in the Girl Scout salute and promised.

"Okay," Sam said. "Here's what you just promised. No matter what advice I give you, you do the opposite!"

"Oh, Sam," Emma said, laughing, "you know a lot more than you think you do."

"Yeah, right," Sam scoffed. "I am the babe with no boyfriend at all, remember?"

"But that's because—" Emma began.

"Hey," Sam interrupted. "No 'buts,' Emma Cresswell. You promised!"

"Okay, I promised," Emma agreed, shaking her head.

"Cool," Sam commented. "Now, here's my advice. Call up Diana and beg to confide your deepest secrets to her. Tell her only she can

16

guide you and your wounded, tortured heart!"

Emma laughed. "My wounded, tortured heart?"

Sam gave Emma a regal look. "I thought it was poetic."

"Oh, it was," Emma assured her. "And that's the advice I'm not supposed to follow?"

"Right," Sam said seriously. "And after that, tell Diana that you are simply too distraught to continue with the Flirts, and that you should be replaced immediately by Lorell Courtland!"

"Lorell!" Emma shrieked, laughing so hard she had to hold her sides. "Oh, my God, can you imagine?"

Lorell was Diana's best friend, and if anything, an even bigger snob than Diana. And she couldn't sing a note.

"That, O Wealthy One, is my advice," Sam finished smugly.

"Sam," Emma gasped when she managed to stop laughing, "I absolutely promise not to follow a word of it!"

"Good," Sam agreed, and she lay back on her chaise lounge triumphantly and closed her eyes. "I'll bill you."

TWO

"I'm not sure this is a very good idea," Emma said to Sam and Carrie, as the three friends dubiously watched a group of girls sailing Frisbees back and forth across the park in the afternoon sun.

"Correction," Sam said. "The interview we did with Kristy wasn't a very good idea. Compared to that, this is a piece of cake."

"Well, why did you go after Diana like that?" Carrie asked Sam. "I mean, you know her by now. She sets you up, and then you fall for it."

"I know, I know," Sam admitted. "It's just that she makes me so mad, it's like I can't help myself!"

"Well, I suggest we just forget about it," Emma said. "There's nothing we can do now, anyway."

"Yeah, forget about it until we see what Kristy writes," Sam said with a sigh. "Then we can kill her and kill Diana, though not necessarily in that order." She watched a girl in bright red cut-offs make a Frisbee catch behind her back. "Wow, great save!" Sam said.

"Whose concept was this, anyway?" Emma asked nervously. "I mean, Ultimate Frisbee?"

"I think it was invented by some kids in New Jersey," Carrie responded with a shrug, still watching the players on the field.

"I don't care who invented it," Emma explained. "I meant, whose idea was it to play today?"

"Darcy's—I already told you," Sam said. "At least, that's who called me."

"Figures," Emma muttered.

Sam turned to Emma. "What does that mean?"

"It means that Darcy is a great athlete, and I've never thrown a Frisbee before in my life."

Now Carrie and Sam both stared at Emma.

"You're kidding," Sam finally said.

"I'm not," Emma insisted.

"But . . . we've played with you on the beach, haven't we?" Sam tried to recall.

Emma shook her head. "I always watched," she admitted. "On purpose. Because I was afraid I'd look like an idiot."

"It's the easiest," Carrie assured her. "Little kids can do it."

"Yes, little kids who grew up doing it," Emma pointed out.

Sam laughed. "Emma, babe, get a grip. You ski the tough runs at . . . whatever that famous ski place is for rich people you told us about—"

"Gstaad," Emma filled in. "In Switzerland."

"Yeah, right," Sam agreed. "And you're afraid to throw a little Frisbee?"

"Okay, I know it's dumb," Emma agreed. "I just don't want to look stupid."

"Darcy can teach you," Carrie suggested. "And speak of the devil, here she comes!"

"Whoa, check out the uni!" Sam crowed.

The three girls stood together on the sideline and watched as a tall, athletic young woman with long dark hair and startling violet eyes approached them, wearing a pair of black Lycra gym shorts, a white T-shirt that read COPE: THE FUTURE OF SUNSET ISLAND, and

21

Nike running shoes. Her hair was tied back Indian-style with a red bandana.

"She looks great," Carrie sighed. "My thighs would look gigunda if I wore those shorts."

"Carrie, Darcy is definitely heavier than you," Sam said.

"She's not heavier," Carrie corrected. "She's bigger. She can pull it off."

Darcy waved and stopped to talk to someone, and Sam studied her. Darcy lived with the Mason family as a companion to sixteen-year-old Molly, who had become a paraplegic after a car accident the summer before. Not only was Darcy feisty and smart, with a disarmingly matter-of-fact manner, but she was also a terrific athlete. In addition, Darcy was somewhat psychic and got weird flashes of ESP from time to time.

She's also the toughest, most self-confident girl I've ever met, Sam thought, as she watched Darcy throw her head back and laugh at what the other girl was saying. *She's nearly as tall as me, but I don't think that I could scare anyone with my muscles. Darcy could, though—and I've seen her do it!*

"Hey," Darcy said easily, as she finished

talking to the other girl and walked over, "glad you guys could make it."

"Emma's regretting it already," Sam cracked. "So how do we play this game?"

"Well, you all know how to throw a Frisbee, right?" Darcy asked.

"Uh, not really," Emma admitted in a low voice.

"Oh, that's cool, I'll show you," Darcy said, and she quickly gave Emma the basics.

"You try," Darcy said finally, handing Emma an orange plastic disk.

Emma cocked her wrist the way Darcy had shown her and threw the Frisbee. It sailed high and arched back around, which was not where Emma had intended it to go.

"Too much snap," Darcy explained, and guided Emma's wrist more carefully. "Try it again."

Emma did, and produced a reasonable throw.

"See, it's not too tough," Darcy said. "Okay, here are the rules for Ultimate Frisbee. We have two thirty-minute halves," Darcy said, spinning a Frisbee on her finger as she talked. "Your team can advance the Frisbee down the field only by passing it. No running with it! When you complete a pass over the goal line, your team gets a point."

"But I can barely throw it—I'll bring my team down," Emma said.

"Nah, you'll pick it up quickly, you'll see," Darcy said easily.

"What if the Frisbee gets knocked down, or you miss your pass?" Carrie asked.

"The other team takes possession," Darcy explained.

"What if you pass out completely and suffer cardiac arrest from running too much?" Sam joked.

"You lie on the field as an obstacle until the end of the half," Darcy joked back. "Then, we bake you into a post-game lasagna."

"Yummy," Sam responded. "I'm hungry already."

"Molly didn't want to come?" Emma asked.

Darcy shrugged. "She's gotten hooked on watching old episodes of *The Twilight Zone*. I couldn't convince her," she said.

"Right about now I wish I was hooked on *The Twilight Zone*, too," Emma said ruefully.

"No way," Darcy said. "You're our secret weapon. No one will actually believe you're playing. Okay. Let's get started." She reached into her pocket and pulled out a referee's whistle, which she blew loudly. At the sound of the whistle, all the girls who were practicing on the field came in to where Darcy was standing.

"Hey, Darcy," Sam asked. "How do you know all these girl athletes?"

"You think only boys like playing sports?" Darcy asked. Then she turned to the group— she was obviously the leader. She divided the fourteen girls standing there into two teams and had one of the teams put on mesh orange T-shirts she had brought with her.

The game started. Darcy was playing on the orange team with Sam, Emma, Carrie, and the other beginners. But the girls caught on quickly, and it wasn't long before they were ranging all over the field like experienced players.

Hey, this is really fun, and it's a big advantage to be tall! Sam thought to herself, as she ran as fast as she could toward a Frisbee that had been thrown by an opposing player to a teammate in the end zone.

Whap! Sam jumped as high as she could and, playing smart defense, smashed the Frisbee with the side of her hand, so that it flew crazily off-target and then fluttered to the ground.

"Great play, Sam!" Darcy yelled from up the field.

"Yeah, I'm turning pro," Sam said immodestly.

"Never, you'd wreck your nails," Carrie teased.

"They're already history," Sam replied, looking ruefully at the tips of her fingers.

All too quickly, the game ended, with Darcy's team scoring a lopsided victory. All the players came to the sidelines to flop on the ground in exhaustion—it was hot out there!—and a cooler filled with soft drinks appeared as if by magic.

"Whew!" Carrie said, wiping her forehead. "I'm sweating big-time."

"Actually," Sam said, "the big story is that Emma's sweating."

"Ha-ha," Emma said. "Anyway, a Cresswell doesn't sweat. According to my mother, a Cresswell 'dews.'"

Sam made a face. "You're kidding."

"Do I ever kid when it comes to my mother?"

"I get your point," Sam said, holding a cold

26

can of Coke against her forehead. "Now, where're the chaise lounges and the island boys to fan me with palm fronds?"

Darcy responded by grabbing a can of soda, shaking it up, and squirting it at Sam.

"You'll pay for this, Laken!" Sam shrieked, shaking up her Coke and aiming for Darcy.

"No, I won't, either," Darcy said with a laugh, feinting away from Sam.

"Eek!" Sam yelled, as the soda in her can bubbled up and caught her in the face.

Everyone fell over laughing, even Sam.

Finally Darcy sat up and hugged her knees to her chest. "Hey, I heard you guys got interviewed for an article in the *Breakers*."

"Oh, God, don't remind me," Sam groaned, flopping back down on the grass.

Darcy raised her eyebrows and looked at Emma. "I thought Sam was the one who wanted to get famous, so why is she upset?"

"The interview didn't exactly go well," Emma explained gently.

"Who told you about it, anyway?" Carrie asked curiously.

"Diana, actually," Darcy said. "Molly and I were at the movies last night, and Diana was there with Lorell."

"The Two-Headed She-Devils From Hell," Sam said darkly. "Molly's parents should write a horror movie about them."

"Well, Diana seemed pretty psyched about the whole interview thing," Darcy said, chewing on a blade of grass.

"Oh, great," Sam moaned. "That should be a clue right there that she's going to come off looking great, and I'm going to come off looking stupid."

"You don't know that," Carrie said. "Diana was really nasty, and Kristy got it all on tape."

"Oh, please," Sam scoffed. "Kristy Powell hates my guts! Don't you remember how she was after Pres last summer?"

"But she's engaged now," Emma reminded Sam.

"Supposedly," Sam said dubiously. "I don't see any engagement announcement in the paper, do you?"

"So, did Diana happen to say when the article was going to be in the paper?" Emma asked Darcy. "We forgot to ask Kristy."

Darcy shook her head. "She did say she hoped it was really soon."

Sam covered her eyes with her hands. "I'm dead meat."

"What is the big deal?" Darcy asked.

"The guys in the band are going to kill me when they see that article," Sam explained, her voice muffled by her hands.

"Sam, you're overreacting," Carrie said. "You told the guys we were being interviewed, right?"

Sam didn't say a word.

Carrie pulled Sam's hands off her face. "Sam? You did tell Billy and Pres, didn't you?"

"Uh . . ." Sam began.

"But we talked about this!" Emma exclaimed. "When Kristy called us about the interview, we all agreed that you'd clear it with the guys!"

"I might have forgotten," Sam said meekly.

"I don't believe this!" Carrie exploded.

Sam sat up quickly. "I meant to," she explained. "I mean, I was going to call Pres. But then I thought that Pres would think I was just calling him because I want him back—which I do—and I didn't want him to think I was so pathetic that I was making up reasons to call him—"

"Calling him about band business is not making up reasons to call him!" Emma voiced.

"I know, I know," Sam agreed. "I'm just explaining what was going on in my head—you know how bizarre it can be—and then after that I kind of . . . sort of . . . forgot."

Everyone was quiet for a moment.

"Well, maybe it's not so bad," Darcy finally said. "I mean, where is it written that you have to get the guys' permission to be interviewed?"

"It's their band," Emma said gloomily. "That's the way they look at it."

"I'm really sorry," Sam said sheepishly. "I totally messed up." She turned to Darcy. "Couldn't you get a nice psychic flash that everything is going to be okay?"

A clap of thunder startled them. Sam looked up and saw how dark the sky had gotten in the last few minutes.

"The only flash I've got is that it's going to rain," Darcy said, getting up from the grass. "Good luck with the article and everything," she added, brushing the grass off her knees.

"It's gonna take more than luck to get me out of this one," Sam predicted.

No one disagreed.

"Hey, looks good," Dan Jacobs said, as Sam carried a huge tray of baked chicken to the dinner table, where Dan and his twin daughters were already sitting. "You've got great color in your cheeks, Sam. What have you been up to?"

"Jocking out this afternoon," Sam replied.

"I'm a vegetarian," Allie Jacobs announced as Sam put the tray down on the table, along with bowls of cole slaw and potato salad.

"Since when?" Becky asked, reaching for a piece of chicken.

"Since eating meat is disgusting," Allie declared. "I think it's immoral to eat meat."

"Since those cowboy boots you have on are made of snakeskin," Becky shot back, "I don't think you have much of a case."

Sam snuck a look at Dan, who seemed oblivious to this argument-in-the-making. He had picked up a newspaper and was reading it at the table, completely deaf to what was going on.

He's a mystery to me, Sam thought. *How can anyone who makes as much money as he does be so out of it?*

"A snake is a reptile, bird-brain, not an animal," Allie shot back at her sister.

"No, *you're* a reptile," Becky replied in a snotty voice.

Were my sister and I as bad as these two? Sam mused. *Well, maybe, but different. Allie and Becky fight, but they also share everything with each other. I can't remember ever actually having a conversation with my younger sister. Not about anything important, anyway. We're just too different.* Sam felt a twinge of sadness, but she shook it off.

"So," Dan Jacobs said briefly, glancing around from behind his newspaper. "How are my girls?"

"Fine," Allie mumbled.

"Okay," Becky said.

"What have you guys been doing?" Dan asked.

"Stuff," they both replied at once.

"Uh-huh," Dan said, and put the newspaper back in place. Sam saw food disappear from his plate and travel behind the paper.

He's getting worse, Sam realized. *He never actually read the paper at dinner before. And this is the only parent these girls have. What a drag.*

There was no more dinner table conversation, until Sam brought out the ice cream for dessert. As she served individual dishes of butter pecan ice cream, she detected a familiar look on the twins' faces.

Uh-oh. I know that look. That's the look that says they're dying to ask me something.

"So, listen," Becky finally said, licking up the last of her ice cream. "We heard that you're getting kicked out of the Flirts."

Sam's heart thudded in her chest. "What are you talking about? Who told you that?"

"Oh, a little birdie told us," Allie said smugly.

"If you want to live to see fifteen, you will elaborate on that," Sam threatened. She looked quickly over at Mr. Jacobs, but he stayed hidden behind his newspaper.

"We saw Diana at the club today," Allie said. "She said you're about to get kicked out of the band."

"Oh, yeah, like she knows," Sam said heatedly. She stood abruptly and gathered up the ice cream dishes. "Like she is a source of true enlightenment."

"She said you dug your own grave in some interview," Becky said with a shrug. "She said the guys in the band were going to be so ticked at you that you'd get fired. She said it would be no great loss, since you can't sing, anyway."

Sam stood up from loading the dishes into the dishwasher. "And as my dearest friends, you defended me, of course," Sam said.

"Not really," Allie replied honestly. "We just listened with an open mind."

Sam couldn't help it. She felt hurt that the twins hadn't stuck up for her. "Look, Diana is poison," she finally said. "You can't believe a word she says."

"So, did you really do this interview?" Becky asked her.

Sam nodded.

"Well, then we *can* believe a word she says," Becky pointed out. "Since that's what she said."

"What I mean is that she twists the truth to suit her own sick little agenda," Sam elaborated.

"Oh, well," Allie said breezily, "everyone does that."

Sam came back over to the table. "No, they don't," she told the twins earnestly. "That is a terrible way to look at life."

"Who cares?" Becky said blithely. "No one listens to anyone, anyway."

"That's not true," Sam insisted.

Dan put his newspaper down and grinned at the three of them. "So, girls," he said cheerfully, "what's new and different?"

Becky gave Sam a jaded look. "You see what I mean?" she said, and to Sam's ears she sounded sad.

Rain pelted against the windows, and Sam could not think of one thing to say that wasn't vacuous, dumb, or totally depressing.

THREE

"Sam!"

Sam slowly opened her eyes at the sound of one of the twins calling her name. She heard a thud-thud-thud up the stairs as the voice grew louder. Sam looked at her bedside clock: 7:15 A.M. She wasn't expected to get up until eight o'clock.

Too early for this redhead! Sam thought, burrowing back under the covers. *I am definitely still off duty.*

"Sam!" Allie exclaimed, peeking around the door.

Sam opened her eyes and stuck her head out from under the covers. "Have you heard about this new concept called knocking?"

"You're in the newspaper!" Allie cried, ignoring Sam's comment.

"With pictures!" added Becky, who poked her head in right behind her sister.

Sam sat up, instantly awake, and pushed a mass of red curls out of her face. "Lemme see."

Allie tossed the morning edition of the Sunset Island *Breakers* right onto Sam's bed. "It's a big article," she said eagerly. "You're, like, famous!"

"You're right on the front page," Becky said eagerly. "At the bottom."

"You're a celebrity!" Allie added. Then both girls cracked up.

"Thank you," Sam replied regally, although her heart was beginning to pound dangerously. *Please, don't let it be a hatchet job,* she prayed. She wasn't about to let the twins see how concerned she was, however, so she just grinned at them confidently. "You guys didn't happen to bring me any coffee to go with my morning paper?"

Allie and Becky both shook their heads.

"Wouldn't it be a kind, considerate, and loving thing to do?" Sam asked sweetly.

"Forget the coffee, Sam," Becky said. "We want to watch you read the article."

"How about if you go get me coffee and then come back and stare at me," Sam suggested. *Actually, I just don't want them to watch me read this if it's really awful,* she thought to herself. *But I'm not about to tell them that.*

"But—" Allie began to protest.

"Bye," Sam said tersely, and turned to the paper.

Allie and Becky headed out of the room. "You're not gonna like it!" Becky called back to Sam.

Sam took a deep breath. *Okay,* she thought, *let's check this out. After that interview, I'm prepared for the worst. Let's see how bad it is.*

Sam quickly read the article. When she was done, she went back to the top and read it again. Then she gulped. Hard.

It wasn't bad.

It was awful.

She read it a third time.

FLIRTING WITH DISASTER?
THE GIRLS OF HOT LOCAL BAND
FLIRTING WITH DANGER

by Kristy Powell

The band may be known as Flirting With Danger, but this reporter wonders whether local heart-throbs Billy Sampson and Tennessee transplant Presley Travis have made a career-ending move by hiring Samantha Bridges, Emma Cresswell, and Diana De Witt to sing backup with the band.

They sound great together. No one's arguing that piece of the puzzle. They brought a sold-out Madison Square Garden Show in New York to its feet not long ago. But these singers don't like each other very much, and it shows. Boy, how it shows.

The question is how long can Sam, Emma, and Diana keep their personal animosity from affecting their music? Rock

> bands come, and rock bands
> go, and the reason most go is
> because the people in the
> bands can't stand each other
> anymore. How long will Billy,
> Pres, and the rest of the guys
> put up with it?

The article went on and on, with liberal
quotes from Emma, Diana, and herself.
And, Sam had to admit it, they sounded as
bitchy as Kristy made them out to be in her
lead.

Sam read to the end of the article and
sighed deeply.

I am in very, very deep doo-doo, she
thought to herself. *It's not even until nearly
the middle that she says that Emma and I get
along great! At least the photos are good. But
Billy and Pres are gonna be livid. We've got a
band meeting this afternoon at Billy's house. I
bet this'll be one topic of discussion.*

Sam looked back up at the photographs. At
least those were excellent. The *Breakers* had
printed one of Carrie's shots on the front
page, above the article, and another one on
the inside. Both of the pictures showed Sam,

Diana, and Emma together, and Sam thought that from their body language, it was pretty obvious that she and Emma didn't want to have a lot to do with Diana De Witt.

Why can't the guys just toss her out of the band? she thought. *Because she can really sing. I hate to admit it, but she's as good a singer as me. Let me correct that. She's a better singer than me. Not that I'd ever admit it publicly. . . .*

The phone in Sam's room rang. She reached for it. It was so early that she didn't even give her usual "Jacobs residence, Sam Bridges speaking" greeting. All she could manage was a gruff "hello."

"Hi, Sam, it's me" came Carrie's voice.

"Did Ian wake you up?" Sam asked her.

Carrie laughed. "How'd you guess?"

"Must be a Lord Whitehead and the Zit People thing," Sam joked without much humor in her voice. "Early-morning paper delivery when their au pairs are trashed on the front page."

"What'd you think of the story?" Carrie asked carefully.

"Um . . . any publicity is good publicity?" Sam said, trying to put the best spin on it.

"I don't know . . ." Carrie began doubtfully.

"Me, either," Sam agreed with a sigh. "I'm trying to think positively. Damn, why didn't I tell Billy and Pres about this ahead of time?"

"You told us you forgot," Carrie said.

"Well, I did," Sam said. "But I shouldn't have."

"I can't argue that."

"I wish you would," Sam groused. "You're not making me feel any more confident about facing the guys."

"Sorry," Carrie replied. "Well, look at it this way. Diana comes off badly in the article, if you ask me. So it's not like you personally wrecked the article."

"It's more like we both did, you mean," Sam translated.

"So, what do you think the guys are going to think?" Carrie asked, a note of concern in her voice.

Sam mustered all the bravado she could. "Our meeting's at one o'clock," she declared. "I'll call you afterward, but I think this'll just blow over. No biggie."

But deep in her heart, Sam was a lot more

worried than she was willing to reveal to Carrie. Or anyone else, for that matter.

At the band meeting at the Flirts' house, Sam sat next to Emma on one of the threadbare couches in the living room, and Diana sat across from them, on another couch, next to Pres. *Entirely too close to Pres,* Sam thought to herself.

At one point she thought that she saw Pres looking at her strangely, but every time she tried to make eye contact with her former boyfriend, he looked away.

Great, Sam thought glumly. *He probably hates me now because of the stupid interview with Kristy. And I don't even need to guess how Sly, our drummer, feels. He's been glaring at me ever since I walked into the room. I wish Billy would hurry up and bring it up because this is agony.*

Sam forced herself to turn her attention back to Billy, who seemed to be talking about everything but the article. At the moment, he was going over their rehearsal schedule for the next week. Then, finally, he was finished.

They all just sat there, looking at one another.

Is he going to just ignore it? Sam asked herself. She looked over at Emma, who just shrugged.

Finally, with seeming reluctance, Billy reached down under his seat and picked up a copy of the *Breakers*. He turned to Pres, who was sitting at a right angle from him.

"Did you clear this interview?" he asked his bandmate.

Pres shook his head no. "Didn't know a thing about it."

"Did someone else in the band clear this interview?" Billy asked in an even voice.

"Yeah, us," Diana said. "We're in the band, and we decided to give the interview."

Billy's eyes narrowed. "Look, we made it really clear when we added you guys as backups that you weren't full voting members of this band."

"Gee, Lord and Master, I guess it slipped my mind," Diana said sweetly.

"I, uh, meant to tell you," Sam said nervously. "I really did. And then I forgot."

"You forgot?" Pres echoed dubiously.

"Yeah, I forgot," Sam repeated, her temper flaring. "Haven't you ever forgotten anything?"

"Don't pick on Sam," Diana said innocently, putting her hand on Pres's jean-clad thigh. "She can't help it if her itty-bitty mind simply cannot retain too much information!"

Pres moved Diana's hand, and Sam gave Diana a malicious grin.

Billy made a low noise under his breath. "From the way you two are acting, I'm beginning to think this article is actually accurate." He stared hard at Diana. "Is it?"

Billy turned to Sam. "Is it accurate?" he asked again.

Sam swallowed hard. "Are you asking whether it's true?" she asked carefully.

"I'm asking whether Kristy misquoted you, or what," Billy said.

"Well, not exactly. . . . " Sam admitted.

"What about you, Emma?" Billy asked.

"No misquotes," Emma replied evenly.

"You, Diana?"

"No, but—"

"Then I don't think there's anything to discuss, is there," Billy said, rather than asked.

Sly Smith could contain himself no longer. He jumped up out of his seat, his skinny frame practically shaking. They all knew

46

that Sly had recently been diagnosed with AIDS, and lately he'd been losing a lot of weight. He didn't have much energy, either, and his previously mature acceptance of his situation seemed to be slipping.

"What do you mean, nothing to discuss?" Sly bellowed. "I mean, what is the deal here? First they give this interview without clearing it, and then they make us all look like idiots!"

Billy smiled. "Hey, it's not that bad," he assured Sly. "Do you really think people aren't going to come to our shows because our backup singers aren't all best friends?"

"No," Sly sputtered, "but—"

"It's good publicity, y'all," Pres chimed in, grinning that familiar grin, which still made Sam's insides turn flip-flops.

O-mi-God, they're not mad! Sam realized jubilantly.

"But they can't go around doing band stuff without clearing it," Sly continued, still agitated.

"Yeah, that's true," Billy agreed. "Next time, make sure you let us know, okay?"

"Okay," Sam agreed, a big grin on her face. "I promise." She looked over at Emma, who also had a huge grin plastered across her face.

"I've got a question," Diana spoke up, crossing her legs sexily. Sam saw Pres's eyes flicker across Diana's bare legs, clad only in tiny cut-off jeans.

"If it's about the interview, we're not interested," Billy started to cut her off.

"It isn't."

"Then go ahead," he said.

"Have you heard anything about the record deal with Polimar?" she asked. "I mean, Sheldon Plotkin was up here and worked with us on the demo and everything, and then—"

"Not a word," Billy said, shrugging.

"No kidding?" Diana marveled. "So you haven't called him or followed up on it or anything?"

"That's not how it's done, Diana," Billy told her.

A strange, knowing look came to Diana's eyes. "Really, Billy?" she asked innocently.

"Yeah," he replied.

"Well, something tells me you're going to hear something from Polimar very, very soon," Diana said.

Pres chuckled. "You been hanging out with

Darcy Laken and getting those psychic flashes?"

"Hang out with that athletic cow?" Diana spat. "Are you kidding?"

"It is amazing the filth that spews out of your mouth, do you know that?" Emma asked in a low voice.

"So, Diana," Sly asked, ignoring Emma's remark, "what makes you so sure we're gonna hear from the label?"

Diana got a beatific smile on her face. "I don't know," she said lightly. "I might not hang out with Darcy, but maybe I am just a little, teeny bit psychic, myself."

When the meeting broke up, Sam rushed back to the Jacobses house to take the twins shopping, and then out to a late-afternoon matinee at Sunset Cinema. Then, she took Becky and Allie out for a pizza dinner. Afterward they went for a walk on the boardwalk—or rather, the twins walked, after begging Sam to stay far away from them so that no one would think they were with their "babysitter."

By the time they got back to the Jacobses, it was nearly eleven o'clock at night. Mr.

Jacobs was still out on a date, and the twins wanted to play Monopoly, which Allie won after a marathon session. Then Sam made them all ice cream sundaes—for once, the twins weren't even fighting—and then she went off to bed. She felt as if she'd been asleep for no more than a few minutes when she heard her name being called.

"Sam!"

Sam opened her sleepy eyes. It was morning. Early morning.

Oh no, I'm trapped in a time warp and the day is starting all over again, she thought to herself. *This is exactly like yesterday, all over again. Tell me I'm in the newspaper again.*

Just like the day before, Allie Jacobs stuck her head inside Sam's room.

"You're late," Sam mumbled sleepily, looking at the clock. "It's 7:20 A.M."

"So funny I forgot to laugh," Allie said.

"Am I in the paper again?"

"If you're going to be such a snot about it, I'm not going to tell you the great news," Allie responded superciliously.

"Yeah, we won't tell you," Becky, who had just appeared in the doorway next to her twin sister, added.

"Great news?" Sam asked.

"The coolest," Allie said.

"I won the lottery," Sam guessed.

"Better than that," Allie responded. "Take a look at this!" She threw the morning *Portland Press Herald* on Sam's bed. Sam picked it up and glanced at the front page.

Hmmm, nothing interesting here, just the usual wars, politics, and crime, she thought.

"What?" Sam asked. "I don't see anything."

"Not there," Allie cried, "turn to the financial pages!"

Sam raised her eyebrows. "You two happened to be glancing through the financial pages?"

"We happen to own stock," Becky said regally. "We know how to read the stock market."

"Great," Sam muttered, "you two own stock and I can't afford to buy pantyhose." She turned to the financial pages as she spoke. "Okay, so what am I supposed to be looking at?"

"Oh, why don't we just tell her," Becky said to her sister.

"Okay," Allie said.

"Tell me *what*?" Sam asked with irritation.

"Just the greatest news in the world," Allie said, her eyes shining.

"So?" Sam asked.

Allie and Becky screamed it at the same time. *"Diana De Witt's father bought Polimar Records!"*

FOUR

"Ha-ha," Sam said, "very hilarious." She snuggled back down into bed. "Good try, girls, I'm going back to sleep."

"Sam," Becky barked, pulling the covers off the older girl. "You're underestimating us, as usual. We're serious musicians, we don't kid about business."

"Read it yourself!" Allie chimed in, thrusting the paper back into Sam's face.

Sam sat up again and looked from one twin's face to the other. *They look entirely too serious,* she thought with trepidation. For the second time in twenty-four hours and seven minutes, Sam found herself doing something that she had only done once before in her life—reading a newspaper before breakfast.

This headline screamed out at her:

CHICAGO REAL ESTATE CONCERN SEEKS TO DIVERSIFY, ACQUIRES RECORD COMPANY

Clinton De Witt, Chief Executive Officer of the Chicago-based real estate company De Witt Enterprises, Inc., today announced the acquisition by his company of Polimar Records, the last remaining major record label not yet acquired by one of the international media conglomerates. "God isn't making any more real estate," De Witt said, "but He sure is making music. We aim to be a part of this growing business."

De Witt Enterprises currently holds title to office buildings and shopping centers all over the United States and Canada. Polimar Records is its first effort to diversify.

"We'll work with the Polimar management team," De Witt said at a press conference, "but we'll also be making some changes."

> Polimar recently sponsored the East Coast tour of local artists Flirting With Danger.

"So, whaddya think?" Allie Jacobs asked, sitting down uninvited on the foot of Sam's bed.

Sam put down the newspaper in a state of total shock. *Now I know what Diana was talking about yesterday,* she realized. *I know what her great secret was. And I don't know if this is good news or bad.*

"She's so happy she can't talk," Becky said to her sister.

"She thinks that the Flirts are now guaranteed a record deal," Becky told her sister. "Well, maybe." She turned to Sam. "Actually, the way I figure it, this is great news for the Zits. Ian thinks so, too."

That got Sam's attention. "How do you know what Ian Templeton thinks? This story just came out," she said.

"We had a band conference call already," Allie reported seriously. She unwrapped a stick of gum and popped it into her mouth.

"Ian called at six-thirty and woke us up," Becky said proudly. "Real musicians have to be ready to move fast."

"Real musicians don't wake up before eleven in the morning," Sam said blearily. She threw herself back down on her bed. *What is this going to mean for the band?* she wondered.

"Hey, before you get all comfortable and everything," Allie said, "we have a favor to ask you."

"Too early for favors," Sam said, feeling a wave of tiredness come over her. She wanted to go back to bed and think about all this.

"Sorry. Here it is," Becky said. "We know that you and Diana De Witt aren't exactly friends—"

That's putting it mildly, Sam thought.

"—but you are business partners," Becky continued.

"And business is business," Allie chimed in.

"So the thing is maybe you could get her to get Shelly Plotkin from Polimar to take a good look at the Zits," Becky suggested hopefully.

"Remember, it's business," Allie reminded Sam.

"I know what business is," Sam snapped.

"No need to get so touchy," Becky said defensively. "It's just a favor."

Sam shook her head. "This is all coming at me too fast. I don't have any idea what the deal is going to be with all this."

"Hey, a member of your band *owns* your record label now!" Becky cried.

"*She* doesn't own it," Sam corrected. "God forbid. Her father owns it. Besides, Ian's dad is about the most powerful rock artist in the world. He can open any doors for you that he wants."

"Well, Ian doesn't want to make it through his dad," Becky said. "He wants to prove he can do it on his own."

Sam laughed. "Come on, Becky, Ian asks his dad to do music stuff for you guys all the time."

"I hate it when you talk like this!" Becky cried. "You sound just like every other grown-up! It is so obnoxious!"

"I'm not a grown-up!" Sam protested.

"Well, you act like one at the worst times." Allie sniffed.

"I'll tell you what," Sam said reluctantly, "I'll think about it."

"That is an answer my father would give," Allie sneered. "The old 'I'll-think-about-it' crap just to get rid of us."

"I'm not. I really will think about it, okay?" Sam said.

"She'll do it!" Allie cried, pumping her fist in the air.

"Wait, I didn't say—"

"We're getting a deal, we're getting a deal," Becky chanted, ignoring Sam. "All we need is for Polimar to see our talent. Sam, you're the greatest!" She leaned over and kissed Sam on the cheek.

Then, before Sam could protest any further, the twins ran out of the room to call Ian and tell him about their big break.

Instead of their usual spot poolside at the country club, Sam, Emma, and Carrie were sitting together at one of the round tables set back from the pool but close enough so that they could each keep half an eye on their respective kids.

The three of them, though, were in deep conversation.

"Have you talked to Billy about it yet?" Sam asked Carrie.

Carrie shook her head. "He left early this morning and won't be back until later," she reported.

"Well, there's a message on the machine calling a band meeting for one this afternoon," Sam said, reaching over and cranking open the table's umbrella to block the direct glare of the sun.

"It could be great news," Carrie pointed out, reaching for her glass of iced tea.

"Or it could be a disaster," Sam countered. "You know Diana. She'll start lording it over everybody!"

"What do you think, Em?" Carrie asked.

Emma shook her head. "Who knows?" she said finally. "Maybe she'll see it as an opportunity for everyone."

Sam snorted contemptuously. "Yeah, and maybe I'm marrying Christian Slater, but I don't think so."

"Hey, I think you would look very cute with Christian Slater," Carrie said with a smile.

"I agree," Sam said. "Now, let's talk about Diana De Witt, the mega-bitch of the Western World, and—" Sam noticed a strange look on Emma's face. "What is it?"

Emma tried to smile, but her lower lip was trembling. "It's silly—"

"Spill it, girlfriend, you're among friends. No De Witts anywhere."

Emma smiled again. "I know this is silly. But . . . well, I was just thinking about when we were all on tour together, and Kurt came with us as the road manager, and, well . . ."

"How happy you were then?" Carrie asked softly.

Emma nodded miserably.

"But you weren't," Sam reminded her. "I mean, maybe you were in some ways, but don't you remember how you and Kurt were fighting, and how he was flirting with Diana just to tick you off?"

"Yeah, I guess," Emma said with a sigh. She rubbed her eyes. "I don't know. I thought I was okay about all this. But lately I seem to be thinking about Kurt more and more." She gave her friends a sad look. "I'm sorry. I know we should be talking about the band . . ."

"But it just doesn't seem that important right now," Carrie put in for her friend.

"You did the right thing, not marrying him," Sam declared.

"I know that," Emma responded softly.

"But it still hurts," Sam declared flatly.

"Yes," Emma said, "still."

"Well, I've got an idea about that," Sam

said, nodding her head. "And we'll talk about it after the band meeting. Okay?"

Emma was silent.

"Okay?" Sam asked again, more insistently.

"Okay," Emma said.

"And don't forget what we agreed," Sam reminded her. "Whatever advice I give you, you do the opposite!"

"Let's cut right to the chase," Billy Sampson said, as the members of the Flirts settled into practically the same seats they'd been in the day before. "There's only one topic on the table today, right?"

"Yeah," Sam cracked, elbowing Emma in the ribs. "Whether we ought to change our direction to chamber music or to rap, right?"

Billy grinned slightly. "Not exactly."

"Diana," Pres drawled, looking over at Diana, who was seated on the same side of the room as Billy and himself, "why don't you fill us all in on what you know."

Diana stood up and stretched languorously, casting a knowing glance at Sam and Emma as if to say, "Don't you wish it was your father who bought the record company?"

"It's pretty simple," she began. "My father has the controlling interest in Polimar now."

"We knew that," Sam muttered under her breath.

"Samantha," Diana trilled, "did you have a comment?"

Sam just shook her head.

"As far as I know," Diana continued, "A&R remains the same. Everything at Polimar remains the same. Except my father's at the top of the heap." She smiled at everyone in the room. "Isn't that nice?"

Sly and Jay traded looks, then Sly spoke up. "So, let's get on with it, already. What's your relationship like with your father?"

Diana looked first at Sly, then at Sam and Emma, superciliousness appearing on her face again. "It's good, Sly," she said. "Real good. I mean, really, really good."

"You mean if—"

"If I suggest something to my father about the music biz, will he listen, is that what you're asking?" Diana asked, this time looking at Pres and Billy.

Sly nodded.

"Yup," Diana said simply.

"So why don't you—"

"Because I don't think we're ready." Diana cut Sly off. "I think we need to make a couple minor adjustments in the band first."

A couple—meaning two—minor adjustments? Sam thought to herself. *Why, that back-stabbing little bitch. I bet she's planning to try to get rid of me and Emma.*

"Hey, just forget it, Diana," Sam yelled, jumping up from the couch. "You think I'm not wise to your little game?"

"What?" Diana asked innocently.

"Emma and I are in the band for good," Sam barked.

Diana raised her eyebrows. "Whatever are you talking about?"

Billy broke in here. "Sam, sit down," Billy said, then he turned to Diana. "Why don't you just explain what you mean."

Diana sat down and launched into a long speech about how she'd brought her father completely up to speed on what was happening with Polimar and Flirting With Danger, and how her father had asked her specifically to be in charge of honing the band's sound.

"You?" Sly asked dubiously.

"Me," Diana confirmed. "The last thing

Daddy told me was, 'When the band sounds its best, we'll finish up the contract right away.'"

"That's great!" Jay said happily.

"Let's get back to the minor adjustments," Billy suggested. "Not that we're gonna do them, but I want to hear what—"

"Actually, there's just one," Diana said sweetly. "Switch me and Sam on the backup parts so that I sing melody and she sings the low harmonies."

That's it? Sam thought. *That's what's going to make the difference between a big-time recording contract and not having one? I might be able to live with that. For a while, anyway.*

Billy nodded his head. "Well, we'll think about it," he said finally, leaning back in his chair.

"Take your time," Diana suggested. "My dad has all the time in the world. If he doesn't sign any other new bands first."

"Tell you what," Pres said. "Give us a chance to talk it over, and we'll holler at y'all later."

"There's no need," Sam spoke up.

"Why?" Diana asked. "Are you quitting the band again because you can't get your way?"

"Diana, chill," Billy warned her.

This time it was Sam's chance to smile innocently. "Look," she said, "I don't mind switching vocal parts if that's what's going to get the band a deal. It's not that big a thing."

"Of course, you'll have to work hard to learn the parts," Diana told Sam. "We all know that singing harmony doesn't come so easily to you."

"I can handle it," Sam said tersely. "I'll work extra hard on learning the parts. I promise."

"Cool," Billy agreed. He looked over at the other guys in the band. "Guys?"

Everyone nodded.

Billy looked at Diana. "Cool with you, Diana?"

"Great," Diana said easily.

"So when will you call your dad?" Sly asked eagerly.

"As soon as I can see that Sam can handle the low vocal parts," Diana responded sweetly.

"That's my call," Billy stepped in to say. "Mine and the band's."

"You're the boss," Diana agreed. But Sam could see the smile on her face was as phony as a three-dollar bill. And there wasn't a damn thing she could do about it.

FIVE

"Okay," Sam said, as she slid into the passenger seat of the Hewitts' car and waited for Emma to start the engine and drive them home from the band meeting, "band business is over. It's time to talk about you."

"But Sam," Emma said, astonishment in her voice, "I can't believe you just let Diana—"

"What?" Sam interrupted, opening the window to let in the sea breeze. "If that's all Diana wants, who am I to burst her little bubble?"

Emma pulled the car out of the driveway and shot Sam a skeptical look.

"Okay, I was relieved she wasn't trying to kick us out of the band," Sam admitted. She looked pensive for a moment. "Hard to believe, though, isn't it?"

Emma nodded in agreement.

"Diana is being entirely too nice," Sam muttered. "Which frankly makes me really, really suspicious."

"Me, too," Emma agreed. "I have a feeling that with Diana absolute power corrupts absolutely."

"What does that mean?" Sam asked, looking idly through the cassette tapes in the box at her feet.

"It means I trust her about as far as I can throw her," Emma translated. "Do you know she actually came up to me and asked me how Kurt was?"

"No!" Sam exclaimed, abandoning her search for a tape.

"Yes," Emma confirmed. "She said she wanted his address so that she could write to him."

"God, she is loathsome," Sam declared. "Lower than loathsome."

"I don't know why it made me feel so awful," Emma continued, stopping the car at a red light. "I mean, things are totally over between me and Kurt. . . ."

"That doesn't stop your heart from having

feelings," Sam declared. "Hey, you have some time now?"

"Some," Emma replied.

"How about going to that overlook near the north side of the cliffs?" Sam answered. "There's hardly anyone ever there."

"To talk about Kurt?" Emma asked. She gave a faint smile. "He's the one who introduced us to that spot."

"You want to talk, don't you?" Sam asked.

"I'm not sure I'm ready to talk about it," Emma said honestly.

"Then we'll sit in blissful silence," Sam decreed, "stare at the ocean, and think great thoughts. And I'll sing old camp songs over and over until you barf."

"Thanks," Emma said, "but no thanks."

"Just my way of breaking the ice," Sam joked.

Emma clicked the radio on, and they drove along the road, listening to a long Mariah Carey set until they came to the cliffs overlook. Then Emma pulled into the parking area, and they sat for a while looking at the cliffs and the deep blue sea below.

"Your brain must hurt from so much thinking," Sam finally said.

"Sometimes I don't feel like I have a brain," Emma murmured, still staring out at the ocean. She turned to Sam. "I know it's crazy. I know it doesn't make any sense. I really, really tried to put this whole thing with Kurt behind me, and I thought I had—"

"Only you thought wrong," Sam said.

"So it seems," Emma agreed in a faraway voice. "What I can't figure out is, if I did the right thing by not marrying him, why do I feel so awful now? Why can't I move on with my life?"

"Move on, as in Adam?" Sam asked, flicking some hair off her face.

Adam was Sam's older half-brother, a film student at U.C.L.A. He and Emma had fallen hard for each other, and Adam was determined to pursue a more serious relationship with Emma. But even though Emma really liked him and was incredibly attracted to him, the whole past relationship with Kurt kept getting in the way of her making any kind of commitment.

"Perhaps Adam," Emma said. "I really like him. But maybe I'm not ready for a real commitment with any guy."

"Maybe," Sam agreed. "Or maybe you just

feel so guilty about what happened with Kurt that you don't think you deserve to be happy now."

Emma smiled. "Sometimes you say the smartest things."

"Don't act so surprised or I'll be insulted," Sam replied.

"How can I ever love anyone again?" Emma cried passionately. "I feel like such an idiot!"

"The thing to do," Sam suggested, "is never to talk to anyone about this ever again."

"What are you talking about?" Emma exploded. "I need to talk to someone who can help me! I feel like I'm losing my mind!"

Sam grinned. "That's what I like to hear," she said. "Remember, you promised to do the opposite of whatever I suggested. Now, if you really want to ignore me, I've got just the person for you to talk to."

"Carrie, I guess," Emma said tentatively.

"Carrie's good," Sam agreed, "but she's still trying to figure out whether or not to do the Wild Thing with Billy—it's not like she's so knowledgeable about guys."

"I'm not talking to Jane Hewitt," Emma declared, naming her employer. "Jane's great, but I'd be too embarrassed."

"How about Irma Miller?" Sam suggested. "Hey, is there any gum in the glove compartment?"

"Who's she?" Emma asked, as she reached over and popped the glove compartment open. To Sam's joy, there were at least a dozen pieces of bubble gum in there, and most of them were still in their wrappers. Sam unwrapped two of them and popped them in her mouth before she answered.

"Remember last summer, when I was having all those problems about the adoption?" Sam asked between chews.

Emma nodded.

"She's the shrink here on the island that I went to talk to."

"Psychotherapist," Emma corrected automatically.

"Whatever," Sam said with exasperation. "I think you catch my drift."

"I don't believe in psychotherapists," Emma said quickly. "I think I have to work out my problems on my own."

"Yeah, right," Sam scoffed. She blew a huge bubble and then popped it with her tongue. "Which is why you and I and Carrie spill our guts to each other all the time."

"That's different!" Emma protested.

"Yeah," Sam agreed, "the difference is that we're not pros. Mrs. Miller is, like, famous or something."

Emma was silent. "It is such an un-Cresswell thing to do," she finally said.

"Well, cool," Sam replied. "You aren't all that big on being a Cresswell, anyway."

Emma was silent again. "I see your point," she said with a sigh. "Lord, my mother would just absolutely die if she thought I was telling some therapist my problems. She'd think I had lost my mind."

Sam laughed. "Kat already thinks you're crazy," she said easily. "And after the little wedding fiasco, she's probably completely convinced."

Emma smiled weakly. "I guess that's true."

"Also, Kat doesn't have to find out," Sam added gently.

"That's true, too."

"If you pay me ten thousand dollars, I promise to keep my mouth shut," Sam offered.

"Sam, you are incorrigible!" Emma said with a laugh.

"To know me is to love me," Sam said

blithely, as she blew another huge pink bubble and then burst it.

"No one else has to know, right?" Emma asked tentatively.

"Your secret is safe with me," Sam promised. "Except for Carrie, I assume."

"Well, of course," Emma said. "Did you really think I was going to hide it from her?"

"Nope," Sam said.

"So . . ." Emma said slowly, "where do I get her number?"

"I thought you were gonna ask for that," Sam responded, "so I came prepared. Here's her number. Actually, I happen to know she has an opening tonight at eight o'clock, in case you want it."

"And just how do you happen to know that?" Emma asked with amusement.

"Well, I might have asked her when she could see my friend, and she of course said my friend had to call, and then I asked when my friend did call when would be the first available time that she could see my friend," Sam babbled. "And she told me tonight at eight."

"I'll think about it," Emma promised, putting the phone number in her pocket.

"Could you call her right away and then think about it?" Sam asked. "I kind of said you would."

"And I feel kind of pushed," Emma replied.

"Yeah, I guess," Sam realized. "Maybe I shouldn't have done it, but I told her you'd call." She threw her bubble gum out the window. "It's a good thing this stuff is biodegradable."

"Okay," Emma finally said. "I'll call."

"Cool," Sam said with a grin. "Now hustle me over to Carrie's house. There's a Zit People practice that starts at three o'clock, and I don't want to miss it."

"You're going *voluntarily*?" Emma asked.

"Yeah, right," Sam answered. "I'd rather staple my tongue to a board. Dan Jacobs asked me to go."

"Too bad," Emma commiserated.

"All in a day's work," Sam responded. "Don't worry, I'm bringing earplugs."

Sam knocked on the front door of Graham Perry Templeton's huge house, and Carrie answered the door right away.

"Hey, girlfriend," Sam said, "practice started yet?"

"They call it rehearsal," Carrie replied, inviting Sam in. "They're all in the basement. Becky and Allie, too."

"Mind if we stay upstairs?" Sam asked.

"That's the plan." Carrie grinned. "There's takeout Chinese food left over."

"A girl who thinks ahead," Sam responded, leading the way into the Templetons' huge kitchen. "My kind of woman."

"It's the room farthest from the basement," Carrie said simply.

"Graham and Claudia around?" Sam asked, as they made their way to the table.

"Nope," Carrie said. "At the beach or something."

"How can Graham go out without being mobbed by a million fans?" Sam wondered out loud, as she reached for the white container filled with cashew-flavored chicken and dumped a liberal helping on a plate.

Carrie shrugged. "Maybe he doesn't look so good in a swimsuit," she suggested.

"Looks good to me," Sam replied.

"Excuse me a sec," Carrie said. "I gotta run to the bathroom."

"I'll hold down the fort," Sam answered, taking a huge bite of chicken.

Carrie had only been gone a moment when the phone rang.

"Templeton residence," Sam answered, grabbing the kitchen extension.

"Hi!" said a male voice that Sam thought she knew but couldn't place. "May I speak with Graham Perry Templeton, please?"

I know that voice, Sam thought, *but where have I heard it before?*

"He's not around," Sam replied. "Can I take a message for him?"

"How 'bout his wife?" the voice asked.

Damn, I know that voice! Who is it? Sam asked herself.

"Not here," Sam responded, swallowing a last bite of chicken. "Can I take a message for them?"

There was silence for a moment, and Sam could hear the voice talking with someone else in the background.

"How about the kid, what's his name— Ian?"

Sam thought a moment. *What if this was a crank call? Let me find out who it is.*

"I'll see if he's around," Sam answered. "Who may I tell him is calling?"

"Tell him," and here the voice got self-important, "it's Sheldon Plotkin, from Polimar Records."

Sheldon Plotkin! He's the head of A&R at Polimar Records! Sam realized. *He's the guy from Polimar who's been working with the Flirts! What in the world does he want to talk to Ian about?* Sam's heart was racing. But she put on her most nonchalant tone.

"Hey, Shelly," Sam said lightly. "You're talking to Sam Bridges. I sing backup with Flirting With Danger."

"Sam!" Shelly exclaimed. "Of course I remember you. You're the blond who looks like Princess Grace!"

Sam grimaced. "Not exactly," she said sweetly. "Tall? Red hair?"

"Of course," Shelly said, "forgive me. What are you doing at Graham's place?"

Sam thought fast. The one thing she wasn't going to say was that she was there as an au pair for a couple of kids in a garage band, and a bad garage band at that.

"Oh, Graham invited me over," Sam answered airily, figuring it wasn't a major lie. "He and Claudia and I are really great friends."

"Oh," Shelly responded. "Listen, do me a

big favor and get Ian. I've got something big to talk to him about."

"You got it."

Just then Carrie came back into the kitchen. Sam quickly explained who was on the phone, and Carrie ran to get Ian. The kid came back upstairs from the basement with Carrie, his eyes shining.

"Listen," he said to Carrie and Sam, "this could be big. But Dad told me to always be careful. Can you guys listen in on the living room phones, just to be sure there're no problems later?"

Sam and Carrie said yes, and Sam marveled that Ian could even think in those terms. Then she recalled how Ian had gotten burned lately by people pretending to be interested in him or his band just because of his father.

Sam and Carrie went to the living room and quietly picked up the two extensions there.

"Hello, this is Ian Templeton," Ian said, in a voice cracking with emotion and nervousness.

"*The* Ian Templeton?" Shelly replied. "*The*

lead singer of Lord Whitehead and the Zit People?"

"Yesss . . ." Ian responded.

"This is Sheldon Plotkin, A&R, Polimar Records. Call me Shelly."

"Okay. Shelly," Ian added nervously.

"So, listen, my man," Shelly continued heartily, "your band is getting quite the hot rep!"

"Is it?" Ian asked, astonished.

"Abso-positively," Shelly insisted. "I've been getting phone calls from all over the country about you."

Sam put her hand over the receiver and looked at Carrie. Carrie had the same astonished look on her face that Sam did.

"You have?" Ian asked.

"Yeah," Shelly said. "I mean, you're like pushing the envelope of rock right off the edge, from what I hear."

"We are?" Ian queried. This time his voice actually squeaked.

"You must know you are!" Shelly cried. "And that's why I want to set up a conference call with you and your parents. Because Polimar is very interested in your band. *Very.*"

"You're kidding," Ian said dully.

"Ian," Shelly said seriously, "about some things, Shelly Plotkin does not kid."

"Wow," Ian breathed. "I mean . . . wow! Wait'll I tell the band!"

"The Zit People are right at the top of my A list!" Shelly maintained.

At the top of his A list? Sam asked herself frantically. *How did that happen? And what about the Flirts?*

Then Sam got a sinking feeling in her stomach as an ugly realization dawned.

I know exactly how this happened. The two ugliest words in the English language. Diana De Witt.

"So here's my number in New York," Shelly told Ian, giving Ian his private office number. "As soon as Graham and your mom come in, call me, okay? *Ciao, amigo!*"

Shelly hung up the phone.

In the kitchen, Ian Templeton screamed with joy.

He ran back to the basement, screaming the same thing over and over again:

"THE ZITS ARE GETTING A DEAL! YES! THE ZITS ARE GETTING A DEAL! YES! THE ZITS ARE GETTING A DEAL!"

SIX

If I hear one more time about how the Zits are just this close to getting a record deal, Sam thought, *I am absolutely going to barf, and I am going to aim it directly at Becky Jacobs.*

Band practice for the Zits broke up not long after Ian ran back downstairs to make his triumphant announcement—the kids were all too excited to continue rehearsal—and Sam had the unenviable chore of escorting Becky and Allie home. Since Sam hadn't brought the car, Carrie drove them; all the way home, all she and Carrie heard about was how much hotter the Zit People were than the Flirts, and about how it would only be a matter of time before Sam would be watching Becky and Allie strutting their stuff on MTV.

"It's not that simple," Sam tried to tell them in the car. "A phone call from an A&R guy doesn't mean anything!"

Becky and Allie smirked at each other. "Do you think someone in this car could be jealous?" Becky asked her sister.

"I'm not jealous," Sam replied hotly. "I'm just trying to help you guys face reality."

"Is Graham Perry's kid the lead singer of *your* band?" Allie asked her pointedly.

Sam had to shake her head no.

Allie chortled triumphantly. "You see, we've got the inside track."

"It's not just connections," Sam said irritably.

"Can't hurt," Becky said smugly. "Besides, we're young, cute and hip." She gave Sam the once-over. "I mean, no offense, Sam, but nineteen is kind of past prime time in the rock world."

"Spare me," Sam muttered.

"I figure they'll start us with a movie soundtrack," Allie rhapsodized. "Something for a really great teen movie starring Jason Priestley or something."

"A movie soundtrack where you guys bang

on the insides of old appliances?" Sam questioned dubiously.

"You just don't get it," Becky said. "The Zits is an attitude. We could be more melodic if we wanted to. We're trying to make a point."

"What is it, exactly?" Sam wondered.

Becky grinned hugely. "You are so jealous! This is the coolest!"

"I am not jealous!" Sam practically screamed.

"We're happy for you guys," Carrie said smoothly, turning the car into the Jacobses' driveway. "We hope things work out for you."

"Oh, they will," Allie assured them. "Ian says he has something new planned," she added significantly.

Newer than industrial music, which consists of smashing old washing machines and clothes dryers with iron pipes? Sam wondered.

"Do tell," Sam mumbled sarcastically.

"What we're gonna do," Becky confided, "is set the poetry of some famous dead poets to industrial music. Ian says it's a sort of point—counterpoint thing."

"Like the beauty of the classics versus the

decline of Western civilization," Allie translated seriously.

Hmmmm, Sam thought to herself. *You know, that's not the world's worst idea. In fact, it actually might work . . . if the Zits had even an ounce of musical talent, which they don't have!*

"What kind of poets?" Carrie asked as she turned off the ignition.

"Dead ones," Allie said.

"Famous dead ones," Becky added. "Ian says then there are no copyright problems."

"Did he mention any names?"

"People I never heard of," Allie responded, shrugging. "William Blake. Some guy named Rambo."

"That would be Rimbaud," Carrie corrected. "Arthur Rimbaud. He was a French poet in the nineteenth century."

"Whatever," Becky said. "Ian says he's great."

"Hey!" Allie cried, craning her neck around. "There's a motorcycle by the side of the house."

Sam, who had been sitting with her eyes closed, opened them. There was only one person that she knew of who might have parked a motorcycle beside Dan Jacobs's house.

Presley Travis. Her ex-boyfriend.

God, I've missed this, Sam thought to herself, clinging to Pres's strong body as they roared along Shore Road on his motorcycle. The two of them leaned as one against the centrifugal force pulling them as they took a tight corner and Pres accelerated out of it.

He said he wanted to talk to me. He said he needed to talk to me. Then he handed me the helmet I always wore. Thank goodness Dan Jacobs was home to say I could go with him for an hour or so. Now, here we are, like we've never been apart. She tightened her arms around Pres's waist and thought that she detected his body relaxing a bit under her hands.

Suddenly, the bike slowed, and Pres pulled off Shore Road into exactly the same overlook where Sam had talked with Emma the day before. The overlook was deserted, except for the two of them. Pres killed the engine. Sam pulled off her helmet.

"Just like old times, huh?" Sam said lightly,

though she actually felt nervous and inse-cure. *I want him back so badly,* she thought to herself. Please let me handle this right. She stared at Pres's familiar, handsome face.

He smiled a wry smile and shook his head. "I can't believe I'm doing this."

"What exactly is it that you're doing?" Sam asked.

Pres ran his hand through his hair, but he didn't answer her question. "Listen," he fi-nally said, "I have to talk to you."

"You're doin' just that," Sam replied, imi-tating his Tennessee drawl.

"There's a great place down there," Pres replied, pointing to an area below them on the cliffs. "I go there with my guitar to write sometimes."

"Cool," Sam replied, "lead the way."

Without taking her hand, Pres started down a narrow pathway that led from the parking area to the cliffs and then down to the ocean below. Sam followed gingerly a few paces behind. A couple of minutes later, Pres turned off the path, and led her to a hollow in some rocks that had a soft sand floor and a gorgeous view of the ocean below.

"Town make-out spot?" Sam asked.

"Wouldn't know," Pres said.

"Can't be," Sam maintained. "No beer bottles or used condoms around."

"Girl, you have a certain earthiness to your nature, did I ever mention that?" Pres reached for Sam's hand and they both sat.

"You may have," Sam acknowledged, leaning back against the rock wall. She took a deep breath of the clean sea air. "Mmmm, it's nice here."

Pres gave her a strange look. "Yeah, it is."

"So," Sam said, careful to keep her voice light and easy, "to what do I owe this surprise visit?"

"I'm not sure," Pres admitted. "When we spent time together at that beach party a while back, I guess I was reminded of how much fun we used to have together. . . ."

"Me, too," Sam agreed. She took a deep breath. "And when you kissed me that night, I thought maybe . . . maybe we were going to try again. But then you never called me or anything. . . ."

Pres stared out into the distance. "I don't want to get into that we're-together/we're-not-together thing we used to do."

"But we don't have to do that—"

89

Pres shook his head. "Sam, you ran a game on me one too many times—"

"I know I made some mistakes," Sam acknowledged. "You did, too, you know!"

"I imagine that's true," Pres agreed in a low voice. "Anyway, I didn't bring you out here to talk about that."

Sam's heart sank and she gulped hard. "You didn't?"

Pres fidgeted uncharacteristically. "I wanted to thank you for what you did yesterday," he muttered, finally.

"What are you talking about—oh, you mean with the band," Sam said, the light dawning.

"Yep," Pres answered.

"Hey," Sam said airily, "I'm a professional artist. I'm doing what's best for the band." *I also didn't have any choice,* Sam added to herself. *Not with Diana pulling the strings.*

"You really did do what's best for the band," Pres agreed. "I was proud of you."

"I didn't do it to make you proud," Sam replied coolly, hurt that Pres didn't appear to want her back after all. "I did it because it was the right thing to do."

"I know that," Pres said. "But it still made me happy. I was impressed."

"Well, maybe you just always underestimated me before," Sam said.

"And maybe you're just growing up," Pres countered.

Sam made a face. "You know, there's something about a guy who is all of three years older than me telling me I'm growing up that makes me want to toss my cookies."

Pres smiled. "Yeah, I guess that did sound kind of awful."

"Anyway," Sam continued, "I refuse to grow up. Don't you hate that phrase—'grow up'? The only one that's worse is 'settle down.'"

Pres chuckled. "Kind of makes you want to get on a Harley and drive off into the sunset, huh?"

Sam nodded and kicked at the sand with her cowboy boot. "So, the reason you came to see me was to tell me I was becoming a model of maturity?"

"In part," Pres answered quietly, his eyes staring off at the sea. "But also because . . . I've missed you."

Yes, yes, yes! "I've missed you, too," Sam said quietly.

"A lot," Pres added.

"A lot a lot," Sam murmured.

Pres looked at Sam quickly, then looked out to sea again. "I was looking for some change in you," Pres whispered. "That's no secret."

"Glad you approve," Sam said, edging closer to him, hoping, praying, that he'd take her in his arms.

And then it happened.

Pres put his arm around Sam and she moved into his warmth. The two of them clung together, as if they had never been apart. Then he kissed her, the softest, sweetest kiss in the world.

Pres pulled away. He had a strange look on his face.

"I shouldn't have done that," he said quietly.

"Why not?" Sam asked him, a bad feeling rushing up into her throat.

"I didn't mean to have that happen," he continued.

Hot blood ran to Sam's face. "What are you talking about?"

"It just happened," Pres said. "It just happened."

"You wanted it to," Sam said tightly. "Otherwise it wouldn't have."

"That's true," Pres said sheepishly.

"So who's playing games now?" she asked him pointedly.

"I'm not—"

"What is the big problem?" Sam cried. "You want me and I want you—"

"It's not that simple—"

"It can be," Sam insisted.

"I can't go back to where we were," Pres insisted. "You flirtin' with everything in pants—"

"But I'm not like that anymore!" Sam insisted.

"What's changed?" Pres asked earnestly.

"Me," Sam said in a low voice. "I've changed." She thought for a moment. "Well, maybe I'm in the process of change, how's that?"

Pres grinned in spite of himself. "More honest, probably."

Sam brushed some sand off her jeans. "So, where does that leave us?" she finally asked.

"We're gonna take it slow," Pres insisted. "Slower than slow, even."

"Okay," Sam agreed. "Slower than slow."

"Almost backwards," Pres replied.

As long as there's hope, Sam thought to herself fervently. *I can take anything as long as there's hope.* "Hey, big guy," Sam said lightly, scrambling to her feet, "I'm in no hurry." She held out her hand to Pres and hoisted him up.

"Neither am I," Pres said, and he wrapped his arms around Sam again.

"I have a feeling this means we're speaking to each other," Sam said solemnly. "I can certainly feel your body speaking to me right now."

"Loud and clear," Pres agreed in a husky voice. He kissed her lightly and pulled away. "Hey, how about we talk business a sec?"

"What's up?"

"Well," he drawled slowly, "me and Billy got a phone call from Diana this morning."

"What did De Bitch want?" Sam asked. "Does she want to fire Billy and install herself as lead singer?"

Pres grinned, then laughed. "Not quite that bad," he said. "But . . ."

"What?"

"She said that she spoke with some people

at Polimar and they want her to take over Emma's solo number," Pres said quietly.

Sam whistled a bit. During the Flirts' tour, Carrie had penned a song that the Flirts had actually tried out, and Billy and the band had decided that since the song was from a woman's perspective, Emma should come forward from her backup spot to sing lead on it. The song had gone over extremely well with audiences. Now, Diana wanted to take over the lead spot!

"*Some* people?" Sam queried warily.

"She was pretty vague," Pres admitted.

"Don't you just know that 'some people' means her dear old dad?" Sam asked. "Or more likely this is what she *told* her dear old dad."

"Yeah, well, same difference in this case," Pres said. "She's got the power."

Sam shuddered. "What an odious thought."

"You think Emma will freak?"

"No," Sam replied honestly. "I would if it was my solo, but Emma will probably be cool about it."

"Yeah, she probably will," Pres agreed. "Emma is . . . well, she's real special, you know?"

"Yeah," Sam agreed, but she didn't like the light she thought she saw in Pres's eyes.

"There's just something about her . . ." Pres mused.

Sam wanted to refocus the conversation. Fast. She cocked her head at Pres. "So does this mean you're going to go along with Diana on this?"

"Yep," Pres said. "It's just not that big a deal."

"It is *too* a big deal!" Sam exploded. "You're letting Diana run the band!"

Here Pres's voice got steely. "Billy and I run the band," he said. "It's not that big a deal because we'll never cut that song on a demo, and we're not doing any live dates for a while. So chill."

Sam folded her arms. "I think this is dangerous. How do you know what Diana will ask for next?"

"I don't," Pres admitted. "But we have to pick our times to make a stand, and Billy and I don't think this is it."

Sam sighed dubiously. "I'm not convinced. Guess who called Ian while I was over at the Templetons? Shelly Plotkin, that's who."

Pres looked surprised. "About what?"

"About the Zits, if you can believe that," Sam said. "Good ol' Shelly told Ian that the Zits were at the top of his A list. Well, you want to know what I think? I think that's the voice of Diana speaking!"

"You think Diana set that up?" Pres asked. "But why?"

"Just to tick me off," Sam maintained.

Pres laughed. "Oh, come on, that's paranoid, girl."

"It isn't," Sam insisted. "You guys never want to believe how truly evil Diana can be—"

"And I think you give her way too much credit," Pres said.

"Really?" Sam asked. "Well, time will tell. But don't say I didn't warn you."

They walked back up the hill to Pres's bike and rode back toward the Jacobses' house. When Sam closed her eyes against the wind a really scary image popped into her mind. It was the CD cover for the Flirts' first Polimar release.

Sam and Emma were nowhere in sight. And the title of the band on the cover art was *Flirting With Diana*.

SEVEN

"Here's what I want to know," Sam said to Carrie as she spread a napkin on her lap. "Are you and Billy going to do it or not?"

It was the next morning, and Carrie had called Emma and Sam and suggested that they all meet for breakfast.

Sam had to smile at how differently the three of them had chosen to dress for the meal. Carrie had on baggy jeans and a white T-shirt covered by a flannel shirt; Emma had on wide-legged white raw silk pants with a short, billowy pink-and-white striped raw silk shirt that ended just above her navel; and Sam had on tiny Daisy Duke cut-offs, a bra top covered with Mickey and Minnie Mouses dancing together, over which she wore a very short black motorcycle jacket that she'd found at a second-hand store. And, of course, she had her red cowboy boots on her feet.

"This is supposed to be breakfast," Carrie reminded Sam with a laugh, "not a scene out of *True Confessions*."

Sam's eyebrows shot up. "What does that mean? You already did it? For real?"

"No, we didn't," Carrie admitted, "and yes, we're talking about it."

Sam made a noise of disgust. "Do you realize that if you spent half as much time actually having sex as you spend talking about having sex you'd end up in the *Guinness Book of World Records*?"

"Well, we only just found out that Billy's okay," Carrie pointed out. "I mean, we thought he was so sick. . . ."

"That was awful," Emma said with a shudder.

"And the whole thing with Sly . . ." Carrie continued.

Sam took a sip of water and set her glass down. "You know, I forget he has AIDS. Does that sound terrible? I mean, we'll all be at a band meeting or something, and I don't even think about it. I get just as irritated with him as I ever did over something or other, and then—*boom*—I remember."

"He looks like he's still losing weight to me," Emma said, worry etched across her brow.

"To me, too," Sam agreed. They were all quiet for a moment. "Kind of puts stuff into perspective, huh?" she finally added.

"Hey," Carrie exclaimed. "Sly is the first one to always tell us to concentrate on living, right? So let's not dwell on all this stuff we can't do anything about right now, okay?"

"Okay," Sam agreed. "You know, I can't remember the last time the three of us met for breakfast."

"I can't remember the last time the three of us had the same day off," Carrie replied, unfolding her napkin onto her lap.

"I can," Emma said, taking a sip from the glass of cold water in front of her and looking out on the calm bay to her left.

"Yeah, about a century ago," Sam joked. "Whose idea was it to do breakfast, anyway? And what am I actually doing up at this hour?"

"Mine," Carrie replied. "I'll take the credit

for this concept of breakfast on the bay. How romantic!"

"I wouldn't exactly call the Bay View the pinnacle of romance," Sam sniffed, looking around at the square tables covered in oil-cloth and the pop-art posters taped to the walls. *Unless I was here with Pres, that is.* Sam reached for a plum that was in a fruit bowl on their table.

"The way I figure it, there are only two things this babe should be doing this early in the day, and both of them involve my bed."

"You are all talk," Carrie hooted.

"Kindly shut up," Sam replied loftily. "A girl can dream, right?"

"You guys ready to order?" the waiter asked diffidently. He was thirtyish, with long, stringy hair and a sour expression. He wore a tie-dyed shirt, white drawstring pants, and Birkenstock sandals.

They ordered quickly and the waiter walked away.

"Your dreamguy, Emma!" Sam cried in a breathy voice.

Emma shot Sam a frosty look.

"Hey, not even your best 'Kat' face can deter me today," Sam said. She leaned in close to her friends. "Guess who took me on a bike ride yesterday, and told me he missed me. A lot."

Emma and Carrie grinned. "No kidding," Carrie marveled.

"And, fellow foxes, listen to this," Sam continued with excitement. "He wants us to try again."

"Sam, that's fabulous!" Carrie cried.

"Well, he says we have to take it slow," Sam amended. "Really slow. But it's progress, right?"

"We're really happy for you," Carrie said warmly.

"Right," Emma agreed softly.

Sam looked at her sharply. "Are you sure?"

"Of course," Emma replied, slightly flustered.

"You don't . . . I mean, it would be silly for me to think that you had any designs on Pres, right?" Sam asked Emma.

"Of course," Emma said again.

"But you like him," Sam pressed.

"Yes, I like him," Emma said, "and no, I'm not interested in him any more than he's interested in me."

Yeah, sometimes that's exactly what I'm

afraid of, Sam thought to herself, but she didn't say a word.

The waiter brought their food and set it on the table. As usual, Sam had ordered twice as much as her friends.

Emma took a bite of her English muffin and sighed with contentment. "This is delicious. Isn't it a great morning?"

"What are you so perky about?" Carrie asked.

"Hey, I bet it's because she got her head shrunk last night!" Sam said.

"That's right, you called and told me you were going to see that therapist," Carrie recalled. "So, what happened?"

"I think it went . . . pretty well," Emma said.

"Pretty well?" Sam echoed. "Please girl-friend, I want details. Details!"

"Mrs. Miller said I don't need to talk about this with anyone if I don't want to," Emma stated, sipping her tea.

"Of course you don't have to," Sam said broadly. "But you want to! Right, Emma-bo-bemma?" She smiled her most ingratiating smile.

Emma smiled back. "No, not really," she

answered. "But if I don't, you'll torment me forever."

"That's true," Sam agreed solemnly. "So?"

"She's nice," Emma managed.

"That's all you can say?" Sam exploded. "She's *nice?* Didn't you get into any of the good stuff?"

"Well, we talked," Emma said, "about a lot of things. She asked me about why I said yes to Kurt when he proposed in the first place, and about how my thinking changed later on—things like that."

"Go on," Sam encouraged.

"She asked me why I'm so embarrassed now about what happened," Emma continued, "and what I expected by getting married."

"And . . ."

"And . . . we talked about my mother," Emma concluded.

Sam looked confused. "How did you go from talking about Kurt and your almost-marriage to your infamous mother?"

"I suppose Mrs. Miller thinks the whole thing is connected somehow," Emma said awkwardly.

"So what did you say?" Sam prompted.

"It's private," Emma replied quietly. "I don't feel like talking about it now."

"Sam," Carrie chimed in, "maybe it's time to change the subject to—"

"I'm sorry," Emma interrupted. "I'm not trying to shut you guys out. I just . . . I need some time, okay?"

"Yeah, okay," Sam agreed. "I'm half-kidding when I insist you tell me everything, you know."

"But the other half of you is completely serious," Emma said with a smile.

"Well, yeah," Sam agreed, forking up the last of her omelet. "So tell me this at least. Did she help you?"

"I think so."

"Then make another appointment," Sam counseled. "Or wait, I'm supposed to tell you never to see her again so that you'll do the opposite." Sam took a final sip of coffee. "Anyhow, I may need to make an appointment with the head-shrinker myself."

"You?" Carrie joked. "You have problems?"

"Remind me never to go anywhere with the two of you this early," Sam said. "You're both too perky."

"So what do you need to talk to Mrs. Miller

about?" Emma asked. "More about your adoption?"

"More about Pres, actually," Sam admitted. She looked at her friends earnestly. "I really, really, really want him back. And . . . I'm afraid I'll blow it—know what I mean? I'm afraid I'll play some stupid game and then I'll never, ever have another shot with him."

"Wow, Sam," Carrie marveled, "that is so mature you're scaring me."

"What exactly are you afraid of?" Emma asked with interest.

"Unlike you, I'll tell all," Sam promised, "but first let's get the check and get out of here. My bod hasn't seen the beach in three days. You guys brought bathing suits, right?"

"Right," Carrie and Emma replied.

"Good," Sam said. "Let's go break a few hearts."

"Ah, much better," Sam said, luxuriating in a new orange bikini while stretched out on her black-and-white–checked bathtowel in the late-morning Sunset Island sun. Mr. Jacobs had offered to buy her a bathing suit at the Cheap Boutique the last time she'd taken the twins in for a shopping spree.

107

"Mmm, the sun feels great," Carrie said, slipping on her sunglasses. "It's amazing how cool it is in the early morning, and then how hot it gets a couple of hours later."

"Speaking of hot," Sam remarked, "check out the next blanket over."

Carrie and Emma looked over to their right, where two guys in baggy shorts were spreading suntan lotion across their golden, well-muscled chests. One guy was blond, the other dark-haired. Sam caught the eye of the blond and gave him a little wave. He grinned and waved back.

"Isn't this exactly the kind of behavior you're trying to stop?" Emma pointed out.

"But this is harmless!" Sam protested. "I mean, being true to someone doesn't make you *dead*, does it?"

"Pres told you the latest about Diana, right?" Emma asked, ignoring Sam's remark and turning over to sun her back.

"What's that?" Carrie asked.

"Billy didn't tell you?"

"I haven't talked to him since the day before yesterday," Carrie replied, rolling herself over to face Sam.

"Whoa, baby," Sam said. "You'd better sit down . . . oh, I guess you already are."

"What'd she do this time?" Carrie asked.

"Why don't you tell her, Emma?" Sam suggested. "You're the one it affected."

"Diana told the band they had to give her my solo number on the song you wrote," Emma said.

"What?!" Carrie cried. "But you're the one who's been singing it all this time! I meant for you to sing it, not her!"

"Diana insisted," Emma said with a shrug. "And I guess Billy and Pres thought it was the best thing for the band."

"You didn't say anything?" Carrie exclaimed. "That really pisses me off."

"Don't be mad at me, Carrie," Emma defended herself. "I'm trying to do the best thing for the band."

"I'm not mad at you," Carrie replied. "I'm mad at Diana. I really cannot stand her."

"Ditto," Sam said. "But just keep in mind that the Flirts—your boyfriend's band—will get a record deal because of her."

"You guys would have gotten a deal, anyway," Carrie insisted. "You don't need Diana to do that."

"Maybe she's speeding up the process?" Emma asked tentatively.

"I don't trust her for one red-hot minute," Carrie fumed. "And I want you to sing my song!"

Wow, Sam thought, *I don't think I've ever seen Carrie this mad about anything.*

"Sorry," a familiar voice said to them from behind, "but that's just not the way it's going to be."

All three girls whirled simultaneously to look at Diana De Witt, standing ten feet away from them in a sleek black one-piece suit with high-cut legs. Standing beside her was her best friend, Lorell Courtland, looking good in an aqua-blue bikini with a ruffled top.

"Hey, y'all!" Lorell trilled in her sickeningly sweet accent. "I understand y'all are employed by my best friend now!"

"Hardly," Sam muttered.

"I can't wait to hear Diana do that solo number," Lorell continued blithely. "I always thought you were just a mite flat when you sang it, Emma, but I never did want to hurt your feelings."

"How kind of you," Emma said frostily.

110

"Emma sang that song great," Carrie seethed.

"That's not how Daddy sees it," Diana said, waving a large manila envelope around in her hand.

"How long did you have to whine before your father bought the record company just to shut you up?" Carrie snapped at Diana. "And what the hell is that stupid envelope you keep sticking in my face?"

"Carrie, Carrie, Carrie," Diana chuckled, her glee readily apparent. "Imagine one as mature and level-headed as you getting all bent out of shape over trifles."

"This is not a trifle," Carrie said. "I'm not going to let the band do my song anymore if Emma can't sing it."

"No great loss," Diana said with a shrug. "I never thought it was very good, anyway. And they'll be lots of other songs for me to sing. Songs I'm cowriting with Pres."

"You said that in the interview," Sam reminded her. "I sure haven't heard about this from Pres, by the way."

"Guess what, Sam?" Diana said. "Pres has lots of little secrets from you. And I happen to have Pres in the palm of my hand."

"Yeah, right," Sam scoffed. "You are totally full of it."

"You think so?" Diana asked. "Well, it just so happens I know what's in this envelope, and you guys don't."

Emma's curiosity got the better of her. "What's that?" she asked.

Diana dramatically opened the manila envelope and pulled out a large sheaf of typewritten papers. She handed them ceremoniously to Sam. Sam took it and read the cover page. The words FIRST DRAFT were stamped in big blue letters across the top of it.

RECORDING CONTRACT
Polimar Records, Incorporated
Artist: Flirting With Danger

My God, Sam thought. *I can't believe it. It's the actual recording contract for the Flirts!*

"Have Pres and Billy seen this yet?" Sam asked.

"I'm bringing it to the guys now," Diana said smugly, taking the documents back from Sam and putting them in the envelope. "But then Lorell and I saw you guys and we just had to stop over and share the good news."

"Thanks," Emma said evenly.

"You could show a little more enthusiasm," Lorell suggested. "Diana just got y'all a huge break!"

"Well, I'm sure Pres will be eager to show me how grateful he is," Diana said, slipping the envelope under her arm. "See you guys later."

Diana and Lorell began to walk away, but then Diana turned back. "Oh, one more thing."

The girls waited warily.

"You shouldn't have said such nasty things about me in that interview, Sam," Diana said coolly. "You never know who's going to be signing your paycheck for the band in the future—know what I mean?"

EIGHT

"This is too cool," Sly exclaimed, as he quickly read over a sheet titled SUMMARY OF RECORDING CONTRACT. "Polimar's going to pay for everything!"

"Looks that way," Billy agreed, nodding his head thoughtfully.

Billy and Pres and the rest of the band, including Sam, Emma, and Diana, had assembled at the Flirts' house for a quick pre-dinner meeting to discuss what to do about the contract offer. Sam was nervous and wary, certain that Diana had something terrible planned. Still, the whole thing about the contract was on the level.

"I don't see demo costs listed here," Jay Bailey, the keyboard player, noted.

"Down at the bottom," Diana spoke up

knowledgeably, as if she had drafted the documents herself. "Right there with rehearsal costs, music preparation—"

"I see it now," Jay noted, his eyes scanning the page.

I wouldn't be surprised if Diana arranged it so that Polimar will pay college tuition for the band's future grandchildren, Sam thought to herself. *Providing they're hers, of course.*

"You know how long I've been waiting for this to happen?" Sly said, a look of pure joy spreading across his face. "Then when I got sick, I thought maybe it never would happen for me—"

"We know, man," Pres said quietly, patting Sly's arm.

"How can they afford to do all this?" Sam asked warily. *I just know there's a catch to all this.*

"We—I mean they—are pretty sure that we're gonna earn it back quickly," Diana explained.

"Hold the phone!" Sam exclaimed. "Are you saying this is, like, a *loan*? We have to pay them back?"

"Sam, if you weren't so ignorant, you would

116

know that this is how it's done," Diana said smoothly.

Sam looked skeptical.

"She's right," Pres confirmed. "This is all an advance to us, and if we make Polimar any money, they get their advance back first."

"*When* we make money, not *if* we make money," Diana stated. "I'm sure Polimar is going to bust their butts for our band."

"Great!" Sly commented. "Because all we need is a real shot, you know? I mean, we're really good—"

"We are," Diana agreed. "I have some plans, but basically we're there."

Sly went on and on with Diana about plans for the band, while Sam eyed all the guys warily. Diana was talking as if the Flirts was her band, and no one was saying a word. Sam looked at Emma, who shrugged helplessly.

This truly sucks, Sam thought. *If I say anything, the whole deal could blow up in our faces. But I can't believe everyone is letting her get away with this! It's disgusting, but I think I've been trumped by Diana De Witt, and there's nothing I can do about it.*

"Hey, not to rain on your parade," Billy said, breaking gently into Sly's revelry, "but the first thing we need to do is get us a music lawyer."

"That won't be necessary," Diana said sweetly. "Do you think my father—I mean Polimar—would do anything unfair to us?"

"That's not the point," Pres responded immediately. "What we need is independent representation. I don't care if the United States Supreme Court drafted the contract."

Sam looked at Diana. Diana was still smiling, but Sam could detect real anger in her eyes.

"Do you honestly think my father is going to rip us off?" Diana asked in a steely voice.

Billy held his ground. "Some lawyer at Polimar drew this up with Polimar's best interests in mind," he said matter-of-factly, "and some lawyer that we hire is going to check it out from our point of view."

Then Diana's demeanor changed. "Well," she said, "I'm sure my father can recommend someone to us."

"Thanks Diana," Billy responded, "but no thanks. I want the lawyer to be from outside the family."

Emma spoke up. "I can talk to Jeff and

Jane Hewitt—they're both lawyers," she suggested.

"Mind your own business," Diana snapped. "You're not in the band."

"Neither are you," Sam snapped before she could stop herself.

Diana raised her eyebrows. "I'd watch my ignorant little butt if I were you," she said coldly.

"I like Emma's idea," Billy said, ignoring Diana's comment.

Sam was seething. *Diana is getting away with murder and no one is going to stop her!* she realized.

"Everyone in agreement about the lawyer thing?" Billy asked the group. "We talk to Jane and Jeff Hewitt?" Everyone except for Diana nodded in agreement. "So look, why don't I call—"

"Hey, wait, I have a better idea!" Sam said impetuously, interrupting Billy.

"You have an idea?" Diana asked. "How novel. I know—you've decided to get breast implants, am I right?"

"When you get a mind transplant," Sam spat at Diana.

"Your idea, Sam?" Billy prompted, once

again ignoring the back-biting between Diana and Sam. He reached over and cracked open a Coke that was sitting on the table.

"My idea," Sam began, looking at everyone except Diana, "is that we should talk to Carrie, and I'm sure she can get us to see Graham Perry Templeton. I bet Graham would put us in touch with his lawyer."

"That's a great idea," Pres said approvingly. "I bet there's nothing in this business that Graham hasn't seen."

"It's a terrible idea," Diana argued. "Do you want to tick my father off? He isn't going to be happy to hear that you don't trust him."

"Is that a threat?" Jay asked with concern.

"No," Diana replied, "just reality."

"I think Sam's idea is really good," Billy said. Diana scowled but Billy ignored her, much to Sam's delight. "Any objections?"

There were none.

"You two are appointed Flirts emissaries to Graham Templeton," Billy said, nodding at Emma and Sam. "Okay?"

"Okay," Sam agreed. Emma nodded, too.

"Now, any other band business we need to discuss?"

"One thing," Diana spoke up, reaching under her chair for her pocketbook and fumbling for a piece of paper.

"So what is it?" Billy said, looking at his watch. "We don't have much time."

"Lorell and I wrote a song," Diana announced sweetly.

Oh God, Sam thought, *and now she's going to tell the band that they've got to perform it.*

And that is exactly what Diana did.

"It's called 'Pop Tarts,'" Diana cooed, "and I've already run the lyrics by my dad. He thinks they're great!"

"I think you should run stuff by us, not your dad," Sly told Diana.

She shrugged prettily. "The song is very hot. You're all gonna love it."

"Yeah, I bet," Sam said under her breath.

"We'll consider the song the same way we consider any new song," Billy said evenly.

"That's all I'm asking for," Diana assured him. "But of course, if the head of Polimar Records insisted that the song go on the album—"

"Unh-uh, Diana," Pres cut her off. "We don't play that game."

"Game?" Diana repeated, looking puzzled.

121

"The band decides on material," Billy insisted. "Period."

"Sure," Diana agreed.

But Sam knew that look in Diana's eyes only too well. *I have a sinking feeling that "Pop Tarts"—whatever the hell that is—is going on our album,* Sam thought glumly. *And I have a feeling I know just who is going to be singing it, too.*

"You're sure it's a legit contract?" Graham Templeton said, as he relaxed in his favorite easy chair in his office in the Templetons' mansion. Carrie, Sam, and Emma sat together on one of the gray leather couches.

Sam looked around the room. The wall was covered from floor to ceiling with gold and platinum albums, spanning Graham's two-decade career as one of the most famous rock and roll singers in the world. There were also photos of Graham with various presidents—Sam saw one with Jimmy Carter and another with Bill Clinton—and world leaders, and other famous musicians, ranging from Itzhak Perlman to Reba McEntire.

"I saw it," Carrie said. "Billy showed it to me. It sure looked legit to me."

"Then the Flirts are right to look for a lawyer," Graham said, nodding. "I'm sure John Ungard will be happy to look it over."

"Who's he?" Sam asked.

"My attorney," Graham answered. "He works out of Nashville for a firm on Music Row."

"But all that music is country!" Sam protested.

"A good lawyer is a good lawyer, and John knows music law," Graham said simply. He reached for a pad of paper on the coffee table and quickly scribbled Ungard's number on it. He tore off the sheet and handed it to Emma.

"Tell Billy to mention me," Graham continued.

"I will."

"Thanks," Sam added.

"No biggie," Graham responded. "I've always thought the Flirts had it in them. And if it takes De Witt's father buying the company to get a deal—"

Graham didn't need to finish the sentence. Everyone knew exactly what he was talking about. At the beginning of their meeting, he'd told them the story of what a struggle it was to get someone to pay attention to him early in his career.

"You use what you've got," Sam recalled word for word what Graham had said. "And if someone in your band's father owns a record company, you're a fool if you don't hope the father really, really loves his kid."

"I just wish it was anybody's father but Diana's," Carrie moaned.

"But it isn't," Graham said with a shrug. "It's an ugly business, the music business. And there are a lot of great bands out there still playing in dives."

"It's just that she's such a bitch," Sam mumbled under her breath.

Graham smiled. "I heard that, Sam," he said. "Just deal with it. When the band gets its first gold album, you can all tell Diana to go to hell. But until then, you've got this imbalance of power, so be careful."

Sam knew Graham was right. But she also knew that the Flirts' first gold album—or any album, for that matter—was still a long way in the future. Which meant she was going to have to be careful for a long, long time.

*   *   *

Sam saw the familiar motorcycle glinting in the full moonlight in the Jacobses' driveway just as Carrie pulled away after she had dropped Sam back at her employer's house. And her heart skipped a beat.

He's back, she thought. *Pres. He's back to see me.* But she looked all around the driveway for him and didn't see him anywhere. Puzzled, she looked again.

"Over here," a familiar voice called softly. Sam followed the sound of the voice to where Pres was sitting on a blanket that had been left out by mistake under the big willow tree in the corner of the yard. She made her way over to her former—or was it current?—boyfriend.

"Care to join me?" Pres drawled, indicating the blanket with his hand. "I'm watching the firefly show."

"With pleasure," Sam murmured. "Just couldn't stay away from me, could you?"

"To know you is to love you," Pres joked, quoting one of Sam's favorite sayings about herself. "Even if you are impossible."

Damn, he looks fine, Sam thought. *White*

T-shirt, faded jeans, lived-in cowboy boots—yummy.

"My goal in life," Sam said simply, "is to drive you crazy."

Pres grinned. "Girl, I'm here to tell you that you have done that upon occasion," he allowed with a grin. Then his face sobered. "And lately, you've been a true friend, too. To all of us."

"Thanks," Sam said in a low voice, a wonderful, warm feeling crawling up her spine.

"I mean it," Pres continued. "I see how you're paying attention to Emma when she's hurtin'—she told me about it, you know."

Sam felt mixed emotions. Happy that Pres was there, that he was complimenting her, and concerned that Pres and Emma were getting close. Too close.

"And I see how you're dealing with this Polimar business," Pres continued. "It was a great idea to go to Graham."

"I don't trust Diana," Sam explained. "I wasn't about to trust her lawyer, or her father, for that matter."

"Sam," Pres replied, "some things will not change. Diana is one of them."

"I know it," Sam agreed, leaning back on

the blanket so her own V-necked white T-shirt was silhouetted in the moonlight. "Anyway, it's great to have someone to hate."

"As long as it's not me," Pres said softly.

"I could never hate you," Sam said earnestly. "In fact, I—"

Pres cut her off by leaning down and pressing his lips against hers. Sam gave herself up completely to the kiss, wrapping her arms around Pres and kissing him back passionately. Her arms found their way around his strong, muscular back, and she held him as close as she could. Their kisses escalated, until Pres gently pushed Sam down on the blanket, leaned over her and kissed her some more. As his lips traveled from her mouth to her neck to the deep V of her T-shirt, Sam shivered, and then she pulled away.

"What's wrong?" Pres whispered. "Are you okay?"

"God, what's wrong with me?" Sam asked aloud.

"What do you mean?" Pres whispered. "Nothing's wrong, you're right here with me—"

"Oh, Pres," Sam moaned. "I don't mean to do this to you—I mean, I really wanted to—"

"Sssh." Pres hushed her gently. "Just tell me what you're feeling."

"It's the scariest thing," Sam said, on the verge of tears. "It's like—I was just totally overcome by fear, you know? No, I guess you don't know. . . ."

Pres shushed her again. And a small grin played on his lips.

"Why are you laughing when I'm pouring my heart out?" Sam cried.

"I'm not laughing!" Pres insisted. "I'm just happy. Dang, Sam, you just told me the truth about how you feel. The simple, scary truth. You're changing!"

"I am?"

"You sure are," Pres responded, running one of his hands lightly through her hair. "That's the first time you've opened up to me in a really long time about anything that you're feeling."

"It is?"

"Yes, ma'am," Pres replied. "I'm proud of you."

Sam made a face. "That sounds so parental."

Pres laughed. "Well, you know, I can't say I feel parental about you."

Sam shivered in the night air and stared out into the distance. "Did you ever think," she whispered in a scared voice, "did you ever think that if . . . if someone you cared about really, really knew you, that they might not like you so much anymore?"

"Yep," Pres replied softly. "Everyone's scared, Sam. Me included. And everyone's afraid to show it."

Tears came to Sam's eyes. Pres put his arm around her and didn't say a word.

NINE

"I'm stumped," Sam pronounced. "Becky and Allie are acting like they're in the CIA about today's band practice," Sam told Carrie, as the two of them relaxed in the Templetons' state-of-the-art kitchen.

"Ian actually cleaned up his room this morning," Carrie reported. "Trust me, that never happens. And he told his father that if he left the house this afternoon, Ian would never speak to him again."

"I wonder what's going on," Sam mused, trying to push the image of herself and Pres together the night before from her mind. The picture was replaced by an image of the grinning, cherubic face of Sheldon "Call-me-Shelly" Plotkin. "Hey, do you think this has something to do with that phone call from Polimar?"

"I guess it could," Carrie allowed, "although I haven't heard any more about it."

"Well, you know what I say," Sam decided, taking her cowboy boots off the chair in front of her, "when in doubt, eat."

"You're always hungry," Carrie said with a smile.

"Gotta keep the world food economy moving." Sam shrugged. "I haven't eaten since lunch, and it's already"—she checked her watch—"two fifty-five."

"Oh, my God, you could succumb to malnutrition," Carrie teased. She got up, went to the cookie jar, and brought it back to the table. Sam peered inside. "What kind?"

"Peanut butter," Carrie replied. "Chloe made .them, with a little help from yours truly. You want milk?"

"What is a peanut butter cookie without milk?" Sam asked, reaching into the jar.

From downstairs, the two friends could hear Ian and his band—Lord Whitehead and the Zit People—practicing one of their new numbers.

"What is that they're playing?" Sam asked, swallowing a cookie and reaching for another.

"You may find this hard to believe," Carrie said, bringing the milk and two glasses over to the table, "but their latest song is based on John Keats' sonnet 'Ode to a Grecian Urn' . . . done the Zit People way, of course."

"Who's John Keats?" Sam asked, reaching for the milk.

"Like Ian says, a famous dead poet," Carrie told her.

A particularly loud noise emanated from the basement, with lots of banging and yelling.

Sam covered her ears. "I hate that!" she shouted.

"It's not very appealing," Carrie agreed.

"This Keats guy would roll over in his grave if he heard that," Sam said, making a face.

The noise from downstairs grew even louder, with the twins yelling, "Grecian Urn!" rhythmically, and then finally it was quiet.

Sam listened for a second. "Ah, peace." She looked up. "Thank you, God."

The grandfather clock in the living room sounded three o'clock. Ian poked his head up from the basement.

"Anyone here for me?" he asked hopefully.

"Nope," Carrie answered.

"Well," Ian continued, "my father didn't leave, did he? Because someone really important is coming to see me."

"Graham's upstairs—I saw him when I came in," Sam replied. "Or at least he was until you started your last song."

Ian turned a little red. "It's just that you don't understand the beauty of—"

His sentence was interrupted by the doorbell. "I'll get it!" Ian screeched, quickly bounding up the stairs and opening the door.

Sam could see the front door if she leaned back in her chair, which she did, out of curiosity. Ian pulled the door open and revealed a familiar face.

"Sheldon Plotkin, Polimar Records!" said the short, somewhat balding, nerdy-looking man at the door, sticking his hand out to Ian. "Call me Shelly!"

"Wow," Ian breathed.

"Wow," came a chorus of teen voices from behind him. Ian whirled around. The entire band had assembled at the top of the stairs and was watching the scene in the entryway in total wonderment.

"Hi, kids!" Shelly called cheerfully as he stepped into the front hall. "I'll be down to hear you in just a bit."

The kids continued to huddle in the hallway, staring at Shelly.

"Go on down," Ian instructed them. "Shelly and I will be there in a few."

The rest of the Zits reluctantly traipsed back downstairs.

Sam and Carrie traded looks, and then they both got up and went into the front hall.

"Hi, Shelly," Sam spoke up. "Remember me? We met through Flirting With Danger."

"Good band, really good band," Shelly said enthusiastically. "So, what's happening with you guys now?"

"Actually we've been waiting to hear from you to find out," Sam said pointedly.

"Oh, yeah, cool," Shelly agreed. "Well, it's being handled in the office. Everything is cool."

"Cool," Sam echoed in a flat voice.

Shelly grinned and swiped his hand over his mostly bald head. "So, these kids are pretty special, huh?"

"The Zits?" Sam asked, a look of distaste on

her face. Ian shot her a look of pure hate, and she shrugged.

"Very cutting edge, makes New Wave pale, leaves that whole Seattle music thing in the dust, that's what I hear," Shelly reported.

"Yeah, that's us," Ian agreed importantly.

"So, is your dad around?" Shelly asked Ian eagerly.

Ian nodded. "Dad!" he yelled up the stairs. "Hey, Dad! Someone is here to see you!"

Graham came downstairs in his bare feet, clad in old sweatpants and a T-shirt. He saw Shelly and looked at him warily.

"Hi, Graham!" Shelly Plotkin boomed, reaching out to pump Graham's hand heartily. "I'm Sheldon Plotkin, Polimar Records. Call me Shelly. And I have to say it's a real honor to meet you, a real honor."

"What are you doing here?" Graham asked him bluntly.

"Came to catch the Zits in action!" Shelly cried. "Gotta get a jump on the comp, know what I mean?"

"When I talked to you last, you told me you were keeping an eye on my son's band," Graham said, folding his arms. "I didn't think you'd take it so literally."

Shelly looked crestfallen, then looked at Ian. "You didn't tell your dad about our conversation yesterday?" he asked pointedly.

"What conversation?" Graham asked, giving his son a dark look.

Ian looked distinctly uncomfortable. "Uh, the conversation where Shelly called to tell me he was coming to listen to us," he muttered.

Sam looked at Graham. It was obvious to Graham that Shelly's visit was not based entirely on the merit of the band's sound, but he was also concerned about embarrassing his son in front of everyone. Ian didn't have a lot of self-esteem, and Graham knew it.

Graham ran his hand through his hair and sighed. "Look Ian, I don't think there's any problem in letting Shelly check your band out," he said reluctantly.

"Thanks, Dad!" Ian replied, his eyes shining with happiness.

"No business talk, just to listen, right Shelly?" Graham said to Shelly, his steely blue eyes making it clear that he meant business.

"Just to listen!" Shelly agreed, mopping his brow.

Graham nodded. "We'll talk later, Ian," Graham said, turning to go back upstairs. "Carrie and Sam, I'd appreciate it if you could sit in on the show for me." He glanced over at Shelly to see that Shelly knew he was going to be under surveillance.

"Sure thing," Carrie replied.

"Let's rock and roll!" Ian whooped, and led the way downstairs.

"Believe me, Mr. Plotkin—I mean, Shelly," Ian whispered, "you're not going to believe your ears."

"That's what I hear," Shelly replied, clapping Ian on the shoulder.

That's for sure, Shelly, Sam thought. *Do you want your earplugs now or later?*

Sam and Carrie took their usual seats, at the top of the steps, and waited for the show to begin.

Ian turned to Shelly Plotkin, trying to look nonchalant, but with deep concern on his face. The band had just raced through "Ode to a Grecian Urn," done the Zit People way, and the last few wallops on the washing machine and bashings of the clothes dryer were still resounding from the basement walls.

"So . . . what did you think?" Ian asked.

Shelly looked directly at him. He was smiling broadly, but Sam thought she detected a pained expression in his eyes.

"Brilliant!" Shelly cried.

"It is?" Ian replied.

"Just brilliant!" Shelly decreed. "Beyond brilliant! I'll tell you, this band is breaking new ground!"

"We are? I mean, that's right, we are," Ian responded, looking as proud as Sam had ever seen him. He swung around to his band. "Told you," he hissed.

"No other word for it." Shelly grinned. "Fan-cosmo, I am at my most serious here," Shelly continued to assure Ian. "You guys are going to go really far."

"We are?" Becky Jacobs asked eagerly.

"You are," Shelly answered. "What's your name, young lady?"

"Becky Jacobs."

"And I'm her twin sister, Allie," Allie piped up.

"Twins, cute concept," Shelly said, nodding seriously. "It worked for the Nelsons, it can work for you. Well, Becky and Allie Jacobs," Shelly Plotkin said in his most pontificating voice, "in a year, you're not going to be able to go out in public alone."

"Why not?" Becky asked, stumped.

"You'll need bodyguards!" Shelly yelled. "You'll be famous!"

"You mean we're getting a deal?" Ian asked, his voice actually cracking on the last word.

"We are definitely talking deal," Shelly assured Ian. "The Zit People and Polimar Records. Goes together like bacon and eggs."

"Lord Whitehead and the Zit People," Ian hastened to add. Then, he let out a whoop that must have carried all the way to the mainland.

Carrie turned to look at Sam at the exact same moment that Sam turned to look at Carrie. And they both wore expressions that said the same thing: on the basis of talent, the Zits deserved a record deal as much as the wailing tomcats that sometimes kept Sam awake at night when she visited her parents in Kansas.

One thing was totally clear to Sam.

This whole thing was obviously the work of Diana De Witt.

"Unbelievable!" Emma said to Sam and Carrie as they sat together in the Play Café that night. The three friends were hanging out together with Darcy and Molly, and Sam and Carrie had just told them the astonishing story of Shelly Plotkin's visit to hear Lord Whitehead and the Zit People perform.

"If you could call it a performance," Sam had concluded.

"You think this is really going to happen?" Carrie asked Darcy, reaching for the pitcher of iced tea the girls had ordered along with an extra-large pizza with everything on it.

Darcy shrugged. "If you're asking me whether I'm getting any special feelings on this, the answer is no," she said in her usual matter-of-fact tone. "But then, you know I never seem to get psychic flashes when I need them."

"Yeah, only when she doesn't need them," Molly put in, sipping her tea. "It's really a drag!"

"Then we'll just have to wait and see." Emma sighed.

"If Diana is behind this, I'll kill her," Sam muttered, taking a bite from her pizza. "What am I saying? I *know* Diana is behind this!"

Darcy gave Emma an idle look. "I did have a weird dream about you," she said casually.

"Uh-oh," Molly uttered. "Watch out!"

"Something about bad news," Darcy said.

Emma blanched. "How did you know?"

"Just her usual weird mystical self," Molly quipped.

"What happened?" Sam asked Emma.

Emma took a deep breath. "I was going to tell you tomorrow," she said, "because I wasn't ready to talk about it now."

"You don't have to if you don't want to," Carrie assured her.

"Oh, come on," Sam chided, "the cat's out of the bag now. If you don't tell us, none of us will get any sleep tonight, and how fair would that be?"

Emma smiled a little, stirring her straw slowly through the ice in her glass. "Okay," she finally said. "I got a letter today from Kurt's father."

Carrie winced. "Was it awful?"

"Did he threaten to cut you up into little pieces for lobster bait?" Sam asked.

"Practically," Emma admitted. "The best thing he called me was, and I quote, 'a rich bitch who should be ashamed for leading his son on'—end quote."

"Oh, Em," Carrie said, reaching for Emma's hand.

"Did he say anything else?" Molly asked.

"He had a few more choice words for me," Emma continued, the hurt showing in her eyes, "most of which I probably deserved." Tears fell from Emma's eyes, and Sam handed Emma a napkin to wipe them away.

"What are you going to do about it?" Darcy asked.

"I don't know, maybe nothing," Emma admitted, drying her eyes.

"I think you should write him a letter back and give him a piece of your mind!" Sam said. "I mean, he's got a lot of nerve!"

"That's not what I had in mind," Emma said softly, still dabbing at her eyes with the tissues.

"A letter bomb, then?" Sam joked hopefully.

"Do you remember, Sam," Emma said, "when you told me that the best advice you could give me about all this was to do the opposite of whatever you suggested?"

Sam nodded. "But I wasn't always serious!"

Emma gave Sam a look that said she understood. "In this case," she said, "I'm going to follow your advice."

"What do you mean?" Sam asked. "You just said you weren't going to write him back."

"That's just it," Emma answered. "I'm not going to do anything about his letter. He's entitled to his opinion, just like anyone else."

"But—"

"But nothing," Emma continued. "My therapist—Mrs. Miller—said that all sorts of people might come to me to express their opinions, as she put it."

"So?" Sam asked.

"So," Emma replied, "they've got a right to, and I've got a right not to answer them if I don't want to. And unless Kurt's father starts harassing me, I don't want to! And that's that."

The girls sat silently for a moment, looking at Emma.

If I was in the crunch, Sam thought, *would I have that kind of good judgment? I doubt it. I mean, look what my advice was.* And the look on Sam's face turned to pure admiration.

TEN

"Another band meeting?" Sam asked Emma, who had called her while she was preparing breakfast for the twins the next morning. "What is the deal?"

"I don't know," Emma admitted. "Billy called me and asked me to call you. He sounded worried."

"Diana must have arranged for us to lose the record deal," Sam guessed. She held the phone in the crook of her neck and reached into the refrigerator for the orange juice.

"My picture is going to be on the cover of *Sassy*! No, on the cover of *Rolling Stone*!" Becky was yelling.

"Not by yourself, you bozo," Allie screamed. "It's a twin thing—that's what Shelly said. Do you think we should bleach our hair blond?"

"Hold on a sec, Em," Sam said into the phone. "Hey, you two! Hold it down!" she called to the twins. "Sorry Emma, Becky and Allie are planning their future of fame and fortune."

"I still can't believe Shelly Plotkin offered a deal to the Zits," Emma said.

"Me, either, but I witnessed it with my own eyes," Sam replied, getting some glasses from the cupboard.

"Well, I hope we haven't lost ours," Emma said. "Billy said one o'clock. Can you make it?"

Sam considered. "Sure," she said. "I just remembered, the twins are doing some cook-out thing at the club. I can probably drop them off and get away for an hour or so."

"Tell you what," Emma replied, "I'll pick you up at the club at 12:45. And don't forget, we're meeting Carrie at the Play Café at nine tonight."

"You're on," Sam replied. She hung up and thought about what she should wear to the band meeting. *Something that will impress Pres without looking like I'm trying to impress him,* she thought to herself as she brought the cereal and milk over to the table.

Whenever I think about what happened the last time I saw him, I feel scared. And vulnerable. Really scared.

"We're not eating," Becky reported.

"Dare I ask why?" Sam wondered.

"Because we're about to become famous," Allie said. "And we'll be on TV and the cover of magazines. And everyone knows that the camera adds ten pounds."

"Look, it's not going to happen overnight," Sam explained with more patience than she felt. "And as I've told you two a zillion times, you don't need to lose any weight."

"All the new models are really, really thin," Becky said.

"They're built that way, like me," Sam pointed out. "It's just a style. It'll change again, believe me."

"You just don't get it," Becky told Sam loftily. "Sometimes you have to suffer for beauty." She got up and poured herself a cup of black coffee.

Sam sat down and ostentatiously poured herself a bowl of cereal. *And sometimes I have to suffer to work for the monsters,* she thought. *Sometimes I have to suffer a lot.*

                    *   *   *

For the fourth time that week, all the members of Flirting With Danger were assembled in the living room of the Flirts' house. The last person to arrive was Diana. When she walked in—at the stroke of 1:00 P.M.—Billy called the meeting to order.

Sam looked nervously over at Pres, who smiled at her. She smiled back. She'd decided to wear her favorite well-worn jeans and an old button-down black velvet vest she'd found in a second-hand store. She noticed Diana had on jeans, too, but with hers she wore a very low scoop-necked black leotard, which showed off her cleavage. Sam looked down at herself and sighed. *No cleavage—never had any and never will,* she thought glumly. *Oh well, I hope Pres likes me for my true self, and all that rot.*

"Okay, everyone," Billy said in his quiet but commanding voice, "Diana asked me to call this meeting." He nodded at Diana.

"Thank you, Billy," Diana said regally.

"It's your show," Billy continued tersely. "Make it quick. Some of us have other jobs." He glanced at Sam and Emma to underscore his point.

Diana got to her feet. "I've got some bad news," she said dramatically.

"Oh, no," Sly moaned. "They're taking our contract away. I knew it was too good to be true."

"Don't be silly," Diana responded quickly, and Sly let out a sigh of relief.

If it's not about the contract, what then? Sam wondered to herself.

"So what's up?" Pres asked her in his easy drawl.

"Well, as you know," Diana said meaningfully, "some members of this band—specifically two female members—generated some bad press for us a few days ago."

Sam spoke up. "Oh, come on, Diana, you had as much to do with it as anyone."

"This is old business," Billy cut in. "We've settled this issue. Is this what you've called us together to talk about?"

A malicious grin spread over Diana's face. "Oh," she said, with false sincerity, "there's no problem about the article with me."

"So what, then?" Billy asked.

The grin spread further on Diana's face. "The problem's with my father. He doesn't want to risk his money on a band with a couple of psychos."

Sam's throat tightened as she started to see the implications of what Diana was saying.

"How dare you, Diana—" Emma began.

Diana cut her off with a wave of her hand. "So the thing is," she continued, "he wants Sam and Emma out."

"Say *what?*" Pres asked.

"My father wants Sam and Emma out of the band," Diana repeated. "He wants new backup singers."

Sam's jaw hung open.

Diana turned to her. "Sorry guys," she said, "it was an executive decision." She sat back down and crossed her legs, a smug grin written across her face.

"Hold it, hold it, hold it," Sam yelled. "The fighting in that article was between you and me. Emma didn't say anything. You are way out of line."

"But it isn't me!" Diana protested prettily. "You know how close I am to you and Emma, Sam. I'm afraid you two brought this on yourselves!"

That little bitch, Sam seethed, her eyes

narrowed at Diana. *Her father had nothing to do with this. She hates our guts and she figured that she could get rid of us and make us look bad at the same time. This is what she was planning all along!* Sam gulped hard. *What if she's right and she can get away with it?*

"You've been planning this forever," Sam said out loud. "And you arranged for the Zits to get their deal, didn't you?"

Diana grinned. "I knew that one would just kill you," she replied. "Not that I had anything to do with it."

"What if we won't go along with this?" Jay Bailey, the usually mild-mannered keyboard player, asked with uncharacteristic defiance in his voice.

"That's your decision," Diana said sweetly. "But my father made it pretty clear to me that the contract is—how did he put it— *contingent* on our getting new backup singers."

"You won't get away with this," Sam said in a low voice. She looked over at Emma, whose face had gone totally white.

"There's nothing to get away with," Diana said sweetly. "This is all business. I tried to talk him out of it, but I'm afraid I didn't have any luck."

"Yeah, sure you tried to talk him out of it," Sam sneered, jumping to her feet. "Everyone knows this bull came directly from you. You're just hiding behind dear old dad."

"I don't think I have to accept insults from a bony talentless stork who *used* to be in this band," Diana said coolly.

I'm going to kill her, Sam thought, lunging for Diana, but Billy stepped in between them. "Hold it, Sam," he said in a low voice.

"She deserves to die," Sam yelled. "Let me just get one good punch in—"

"Sit," Billy barked at Sam. Sam reluctantly went back to her seat, fuming.

"Diana," Billy said, turning to her, "would you excuse yourself for about five minutes?"

"Why?" Diana asked.

"Because we have something we want to talk about behind your back," Pres drawled. "So git!"

Diana looked like she was about to spit nails but then composed herself. She knew she was holding all the aces in the deck.

"Fine," she said, "I'll be sitting on the front porch." With that, she got up and left.

The band sat in stunned silence for a moment, and then Billy, as usual, took command.

"Well," he said jocularly, "that was an interesting piece of news."

"She's full of crap," Sam snorted. "Her father had nothing to do with this!"

"What difference does it make?" Sly asked. "She has the power, whether we like it or not."

"Not necessarily," Jay said. "There are always two choices in every situation."

Sly's already pale face grew paler. "I've been waiting all my life to get a deal, man," he said. "I'm not turning it down over backup singers, not even backup singers I like."

Billy turned to Pres. "What do you think?" he said to his buddy.

"I think Diana's tryin' to blackmail Sam and Emma out of the band, and I think I don't respond well to blackmail," Pres said evenly, though the color was draining from his face. "It ain't business—it's personal."

"So it's personal," Sly said, his eyes blazing. "That's show biz, right? We were a band before we had backups; we can be a band with a deal with different backups." He looked over at Sam and Emma. "You understand, don't you?"

"No," Sam said bluntly. "Why should I?"

"It's not so simple," Emma murmured. "Besides, how do you know what she'll ask for next?"

Sly folded his arms defensively. "I guess we'd have to take that as it comes."

"So you'd vote to let Sam and Emma go?" Pres asked.

"Sorry," Sly answered, "but yeah. Look, I don't know how much time I've got. This is what I've always dreamed of. It's too big an opportunity." He looked at Sam and Emma again. "Hey, we can hire you guys back when our first record goes platinum."

"How 'bout you, Pres?" Billy asked.

Pres sighed. "Sometimes you just got to stand for something," he said quietly. "It may mean we lose the deal, but I'm not letting Diana De Witt tell us how to run our band."

Sam looked at Pres gratefully. He looked back at her and nodded solemnly. Sam's heart filled with love. *He is the greatest,* she thought. *He's not just doing this to protect me, he's doing this because he's standing up for a principle.*

Billy rubbed his chin thoughtfully for a moment. "I agree," he finally said. "Forget Diana. We'll get a deal some other way."

"Wait a sec," Jay Bailey said, looking over at Sam and Emma as if begging forgiveness in advance for what he was about to say. "I . . . wow, this is hard to say. I gotta agree with Sly. I don't want to, but I do."

Two against two, Sam thought. *Bad odds.*

"How come?" Billy asked him.

"It's too big a chance to let go," Jay said earnestly. "Come on, you guys!" he implored Pres and Billy. "You remember all those dives we've played? You remember all those times we were too broke to eat more than junk food?"

Pres and Billy nodded.

"We've been at this a long time, man," Jay continued. "We've hung together through a whole lot of stuff. Offers like this Polimar thing won't fall into our laps every day. We've got to be practical about this!"

Sly paced around the room. "I've worked my whole life for an opportunity like this." His hands were shaking as he picked a soda up from the table and pulled open the tab. "I can't just let it slip through my fingers!"

Pres went to Sly and touched his arm gently. "I know how you feel—"

"Do you?" Sly asked him sharply. "But how could you?"

"You're right," Pres finally allowed. "I couldn't. But I can't go against what I believe in because of it, Sly."

"We're really good, Sly," Billy said. "We'll get another offer."

Sly looked ready to cry. He turned his back on them and threw back the soda.

"Looks like we're deadlocked," Pres surmised. He looked over at Emma and Sam. "You two have anything you want to say?"

Emma struggled a moment. "It's funny, you know, I never thought I'd be in a band." She looked over at Sam. "I mean, I auditioned because Sam practically forced me to, and I never thought I'd get in." She bit at her lower lip anxiously. "But now, well, the band means a lot to me. And I would really, really miss it. But . . . I'd understand if you voted us out."

Billy smiled at Emma, then he turned to Sam. "Sam?"

"I want to talk to Emma for a minute," she said. "Alone."

Billy raised his eyebrows quizzically, but

then nodded. "Come on guys," he said to his bandmates, and they all exited into the kitchen. With that, Sam turned to Emma.

"De Witt. She's scum," Sam said.

"Lower than scum," Emma agreed.

"Sub-scum," Sam said.

"But what are we going to do?" Emma asked her friend.

"You're looking to me for advice?" Sam replied, unable to stop herself from making a joke even at this serious moment. "Whatever I tell you you're going to do the opposite."

"Not this time," Emma promised.

"Wait'll you hear what I suggest," Sam retorted.

"Look," Emma said to her friend, "I can live without the band. If I have to."

"Elaborate," Sam demanded, picking some nail polish anxiously off her pinky.

"I just . . . well, it was never really my dream, you know," Emma struggled to explain, "and then, there's everything that's going on with Kurt."

Sam looked Emma right in the eye.

"I'm with you," she said quietly.

"You mean—"

"I mean I don't think we should make the

guys have to kick us out," Sam explained. "I think we should quit voluntarily."

"But then Diana will win!" Emma pointed out.

"This round," Sam answered, "but only this round."

Emma gave Sam a look of admiration. "You'd really do that?"

"Yeah," Sam said.

"But you want to be a star!" Emma cried. "And you're giving it up!"

"No, no, no, fellow fox," Sam said, trying for a light tone. "I look at it this way—the Flirts aren't my band, never were, never will be. Some day I'll be a star on my own."

"But that's not why you're doing it," Emma realized. "You're doing it for Pres, and Billy and Jay. And Sly," she added. "A lot of this is about Sly, isn't it?"

"Maybe," Sam conceded. "Who knows how long Sly is going to live? And this means everything to him. Maybe it'll even keep him alive longer."

Emma smiled at Sam. "You are amazing."

"I am, aren't I?" Sam said. She tried hard not to let the tears she felt threatening come to her eyes. "Now let's call the guys back in here before I lose all my nerve."

Emma hugged Sam tightly. "You are the coolest, Sam Bridges. Diana should be ashamed of herself."

"Not likely," Sam commented. "Anyway, someday I will get even."

"I'll go get the guys," Emma offered, leaving the room.

Somehow, some way, some day, Sam thought. *No way is De Witt going to get away with this. No way in the world.*

"Unbelievable," Carrie said, as Emma and Sam told her the story of what had happened with the band earlier that day. "Billy called and told me what you decided, but he didn't tell me how you decided it."

"It was the right thing to do," Emma explained, "but it was really Sam's idea."

"Amazing," Carrie said.

"Not really," Sam replied. "I just did what I thought was right."

Carrie shook her head. "I don't know if I could have been that mature about the whole thing," she admitted. "I would really like to kill Diana for this little scheme."

"You would have been so proud, Carrie. Billy asked me and Em at least three times if we were sure, and we held steady. It was almost worth it just to see the look Pres gave me when he found out what we decided," Sam recalled. She closed her eyes and recalled how he had come over to her and kissed her in front of everyone.

"Well, there's only one solution," Sam continued. "I'm going to have to start my own band." She looked around the crowded room, hoping for a glimpse of the waitress. "Where's our food? I'm starving."

As if on cue Marie weaved her way through the masses carrying a loaded tray heaped with chicken wings, sliced vegetables with dip, loaded potato skins, and a huge pitcher of iced tea.

"Thanks," Sam said over the blaring music, "can you turn the music monitors down? I can barely think in here."

"You want 'em down, the guys at the next table want 'em up," Marie said with a sigh. "How 'bout if I just keep my hand on the dial and turn it up and down, up and down?" She wandered off through the crowd.

"I'd say this job is getting to her," Carrie stated.

"Mmmm, this is so good," Sam said, devouring a chicken wing. "So, listen, you guys, just so you don't think I've turned into Saint Sam or something, how are we going to take Diana down a notch or two?"

"Show up at the auditions for the new backups?" Emma ventured. "They're tomorrow."

"Great idea!" Sam chortled. The girls cracked up. "But I don't think so."

"So, what then?" Carrie asked, reaching for a slice of green pepper. "I don't care what the grown-up thing to do is here, I really want revenge."

"Something will come to me," Sam said, licking some hot sauce off her finger. She looked at Emma. "Won't it be weird not going to band practice? Not having gigs?"

"And watching the Flirts perform?" Emma added sadly.

Sam thought about that for a moment. "You're right," she finally said. "That is going to be awful. Really awful."

Emma smiled ruefully. "What I didn't want was more free time. It just gives me more opportunities to obsess about you-know-who."

"I keep telling you," Sam said. "The smartest decision you ever made was not to marry Kurt."

"Maybe," Emma mused. "Maybe so. But I wonder sometimes."

"Not me," Sam replied with certainty. "And a saint like me should know. What I wonder is how to wreak revenge on Diana. Now, help me think!"

ELEVEN

"Sam, wake up!" Becky hissed at the door to Sam's room.

Sam opened one eye and groaned. "What?"

"We've got to show you something," Allie said, her head visible next to her sister's in the doorway.

Sam squinted at her bedside clock: 7:15 A.M. "Listen, this new early morning thing of yours has got to stop," Sam mumbled, burrowing back under the covers.

"It's important!" Becky insisted. "It's about your band—or should I say, your *former* band."

But how in the world did they find out? Sam wondered sleepily. *I certainly didn't tell them.*

"Go away," Sam told them. "I'm in no mood to talk about it."

"But don't you want to know how we know?" Allie asked.

"No, what I want to know is why you keep waking me up and why you never knock before you invade my room," Sam grumbled in reply.

"It's not our fault if you're famous," Becky said. She and her sister shared a look, and then they both marched into Sam's room. Becky was holding the morning paper.

"I don't know how you do it—" Allie began.

"—but you're front-page news again!" Becky finished, brandishing the paper at Sam.

Sam closed her eyes. *My life is like this déjà vu experience,* she thought. When she opened them, the newspaper was lying on top of her comforter.

Oh hell, Sam thought, reaching for the newspaper, *here we go again.* She looked down to the big boxed article at the right side of the front page and began to read.

MUSICAL CHAIRS ON ISLAND AS FLIRTS SHAKE UP LINE-UP AND ZIT PEOPLE GRAB BRASS RING: POLIMAR RECORDS ZEROS IN ON LOCAL BANDS

by Kristy Powell

It's been a big week on the island for our local music scene. We're talking real big. Huge, even.

Local rockers Flirting With Danger have canned two of their backup singers—which in this reporter's opinion shouldn't really hurt their sound—and have tentatively been offered a recording contract by major label Polimar Records.

Sam Bridges and Emma Cresswell are out. The bloodletting happened yesterday, a source close to the band told this reporter. Reportedly, the Flirts are holding new audi-

167

tions today. Summer island residents Maia Jong and Kimber Averly have got the inside track, according to the source.

Do you think any of this has anything to do with the fact that Diana De Witt, the third backup, and Bridges's and Cresswell's very "best" friend, has a rich father who just bought Polimar Records?

Naah.

Meanwhile, across the island, local industrial-music tyros Lord Whitehead and the Zit People got a visit from the A&R department of, you guessed it, Polimar Records. A&R kingpin Sheldon Plotkin paid a visit to hear the Zits do their thing. And Plotkin, reportedly, was mighty impressed by the wall of sound generated by Ian Templeton's band of industrial bangers.

Do you think any of this has anything to do with the fact

that Ian Templeton, who leads the Zits, is the son of none other than rock legend Graham Perry? Or do we see Diana De Witt's hand in this again, maybe just to get the goat of S.B., who actually babysits for the backup chanters in this kiddie band?

Naah . . .

Sam finished reading the article, lay down on her bed, and pulled her pillow over her head. "I'm never getting up," she announced. "Never, never, never."

Becky gently pulled the pillow off of Sam's face. "Sorry, Sam," she said sincerely. "I know you really cared about the band."

Sam could feel tears coming to her eyes. "Yeah," she admitted.

"Why did it happen?" Allie asked with concern.

"Diana—just like the article says," Sam reported.

"But that is totally unfair!" Becky cried.

"That's show biz," Sam said with a sigh.

Becky put her hands on her hips. "You

mean to tell me that Pres—your *boyfriend*—actually let Diana kick you out of the band?"

"Emma and I decided to bow out on our own," Sam explained. "Otherwise the Flirts would have lost their deal with Polimar."

The twins eyes got very large. "Wow," Becky said. "I don't know if I'd do that."

"You know what I can't stand?" Allie asked. "When stuff is unfair. Diana is being totally unfair." She picked up the paper and gave the article a contemptuous look. "And that Kristy Powell is so bitchy and so unfair," she ranted.

"It's her column—no one can stop her," Sam replied with exhaustion.

"Well, what does she mean about our only getting a deal because of Graham or because Diana wants to make you mad, huh?" Becky demanded.

"Got me," Sam replied. *Okay, so it's a little white lie,* she added to herself.

"We're getting a deal because we're unique and on the cutting edge, right?" Becky asked Sam.

Sam sighed. "I honestly don't know, Becky."

"And that babysitter remark!" Allie exclaimed. "Of all the low, nasty—"

"And she called us a 'kiddie band'!" Becky

added, fuming. "I'd like to punch her lights out!"

"Stand in line," Sam replied.

"We can make our own breakfast if you want to sleep later," Becky offered.

"Thanks," Sam said, suddenly so depressed she couldn't bear the thought of getting out of bed.

The twins headed for the door, then they both turned around.

"The Zits really are good, right?" Allie asked Sam. "I mean, I'm not saying perfect or anything, but . . ."

"You guys are, uh . . . unique," Sam said with as much kindness as she could muster.

"Yeah, and that's why Polimar wants us," Becky told her sister. "Everything is cool." She turned back to Sam. "See ya."

Sam covered her head with her pillow again, her head filled with only one thought: *I hate Diana.*

Carrie, Emma, and Sam had commandeered their usual corner by the main pool of the Sunset Island Country Club. Carrie was there with little Chloe Templeton, Emma was there with Katie Hewitt, and Sam was there with the Jacobs twins.

They'd all arrived about the same time. And they'd all noticed the other people at the pool buzzing and pointing as they made their entrance. Clearly, most everyone had read the *Breakers* that morning and knew what was up.

After they'd gotten the little kids to their swimming lesson—some new girl they didn't know had replaced Kurt Ackerman as head swim instructor, much to Katie Hewitt's dismay—Carrie leaned forward confidentially to talk to her friends.

"I've got some news," she announced.

Sam frowned, smoothing some sunblock on her long legs. "After this morning's paper, I don't think I want any more news," she said glumly.

"Okay," Carrie said nonchalantly, "I won't tell you what Graham told me this morning before we got here."

"News from Graham Perry I can handle," Sam amended. "What's up?"

"Well," Carrie began, "you know that Ian

read the story in the *Breakers* this morning."

"Of course," Sam replied.

"How did he react?" Emma queried.

"Pretty well," Carrie replied. "Ian is convinced the nasty journalist's cracks are the product of a corrupt post-industrial society."

"Wish I felt that way," Sam said with a sigh.

"So anyway," Carrie continued, "Graham read it, too."

"So?" Sam urged.

"It really pissed him off," Carrie said. "I don't think I've ever seen him that mad."

"Mad about Ian or mad about the Flirts?" Emma asked.

"The Flirts," Carrie said. "He wouldn't do anything that would hurt Ian's feelings."

"Big deal," Sam said. "Graham feels bad."

"That's not all," Carrie remarked.

"What else?" Emma asked.

"Well, you know that Graham records for Macro Records, right?" Carrie asked.

Sam and Emma nodded.

"He told me he's going to call their A&R chief about the Flirts," Carrie concluded triumphantly.

"That's great news!" Sam chortled. "We can kick Diana out of the band and—"

"Wait a second," Emma replied, "not so fast. Graham calling Macro and Macro giving the Flirts a deal aren't the same, right?" She looked at Carrie.

Carrie nodded. "Graham said that the head of A&R hasn't signed a new band in two years, but that he'd call anyway."

Sam's face fell. "And there's still the Polimar deal?" she said.

"Right," Carrie replied. "But this is better than nothing."

"Does Billy know?" Emma asked.

"He does now," Carrie responded, repositioning her sunglasses on her nose. "Graham called him."

"Graham called him?" Sam said, astonished. Graham Perry never called anyone.

"Yup," Carrie said. "I was right there listening."

"What was his reaction?" Emma asked.

"Medium," Carrie admitted. "He knows a call to Macro Records and getting signed aren't the same thing. Anyway, I still think this is really good news."

"A little better," Emma agreed.

"Somewhat," Sam answered. "Just somewhat."

"Hey, Sam," Pres's voice came over the phone, "it's me."

"Hold on a sec," Sam answered, getting up from the dinner table. "I'm gonna switch phones." She walked into the living room, picked up the extension there, and yelled at the twins to hang up the phone in the kitchen.

I know they're just dying to listen in, Sam thought.

"Eat your dinner!" Sam yelled again. "And hang up the phone!" Finally, she heard the receiver click down.

"Hi," Sam said into the phone. "The coast is clear."

"What you did—" Pres began.

"What Emma and I did," Sam corrected.

"What you did was incredible," Pres said. "I'm deeply impressed. Billy, too."

"Thanks," Sam said. "I . . ." *Be honest, Sam,* she told herself. *Just be honest.* "It means a lot to me that you feel that way," she finally said.

"I've been thinking about you," Pres said.

"Good stuff?"

"Very," Pres said. "I'd like to tell you in person sometime soon."

Sam took a deep breath. "The auditions were today, weren't they?"

"Yeah," Pres confirmed. "We only saw, like, a dozen girls, all of them recommended by someone."

"So, who'd you pick?" Sam asked, clutching the phone hard.

"Maia Jong and Kimber Averly."

"Wait a second," Sam said, her temper flaring, "that's exactly who Kristy said you guys would pick in her article! And the only way she could know that would be if Diana told her, which means that you guys picked who Diana told you to pick!"

"Sam, we picked the two girls we thought were the best," Pres said in a gentle voice.

Sam gritted her teeth. Maia and Kimber were the last two girls to be eliminated at the Flirts' auditions when Sam and Emma got picked.

It's gonna kill me to see those two up on

stage with Diana, Sam thought. *It's absolutely gonna kill me.*

"Well," Sam forced herself to say, "I hope it works out for you."

"You helped us dodge a bullet," Pres replied.

"Always willing to help," Sam answered. "I just hope Diana doesn't pull any more crap."

Pres was quiet for a moment. "She already has," he said finally.

"Now what?"

"She's asked us—no, she says her father wants us—to put her in the middle of the three backups," Pres explained. "With Maia to her left and Kimber to her right."

"So, that's no biggie," Sam answered, sitting down in one of the upholstered chairs in the Jacobses' living room.

"Well that's not all," Pres continued. "She made a joke today about the title of the first album."

"Do tell," Sam urged.

"She said it should be titled *Flirting With Diana*," Pres said.

"My God, I had a nightmare about that!" Sam exclaimed. "Now even my worst dreams are coming true!"

"Sorry," Pres said. He was quiet for a moment. "I've got a major favor to ask you. You can say no if you want."

"Try me," Sam said.

"We're rehearsing the new backups tomorrow afternoon, and then we're gonna do three tunes at the Play Café tomorrow night, just to begin breaking them in."

"So?"

"I'd like it if you and Emma could be there," Pres murmured. "Carrie, too."

"But why?"

"I'm not sure," Pres admitted. "Maybe to put some pressure on the new girls. But really, I guess, I don't want to see Diana get away with this without having to face y'all."

"Yeah, she'll just love being up there on stage with us out-of-work peons standing below."

"Oh, girl, you can definitely hold your head up high," Pres said. "Diana De Witt can't shine your cowboy boots."

Sam smiled. She felt really good and really sad at the same time. "Pres, we stepped down for the good of the band, but we aren't exactly happy about it. I'll . . . think about it," she said. "How's that?"

"Good enough for me," Pres replied. "I'll be looking for your beautiful face."

TWELVE

"Emma-bo-bemma, as your best friend, I gotta tell you, you look like hell," Sam said brightly, as Emma approached her and Carrie on the beach. The girls had managed to arrange a couple of hours off at the same time and had agreed to try to take advantage of a relatively quiet weekday on the island to soak up some sun.

"What's wrong?" Carrie asked Emma, turning over on her rattan mat to greet her friend.

"Not much," Emma said tremulously. "Just that this is about the worst day of my life."

"Are you sick?" Sam asked, a frightened look on her face.

Emma plopped down next to Sam and tried to smile bravely. "I'm not sick," she assured them.

"So what happened?" Sam asked.

Emma pointed to her purse. "In there are two letters I got today—one from Kurt, and one from your brother, Adam."

Sam grimaced. "Oops."

"Unbelievable," Carrie commented, reaching for her sunglasses.

Emma sighed. She reached into her bag and took out a letter in a rumpled envelope, and handed it to Carrie. It was postmarked from Michigan.

"You want me to read it?" Carrie asked, astonished.

"Go ahead," Emma said. "It's short."

"Read quietly," Sam told her, "Kristy Powell and her spies are everywhere."

"Don't worry," Carrie replied. "We're not ending up in the newspaper with this."

Emma,

It happened. I know it happened. And I still can't believe you did it. I guess you aren't the girl I thought you were, which means I was in love with a fantasy. That breaks my heart. But it should break yours even more. You took our love and threw it away. I'll never be able to forget about you, and I will never be able to forgive you.

Kurt

"Wow," Sam breathed. "It's awful."

"What are you going to do?" Carrie asked, handing Emma back the letter.

"Make another appointment with Mrs. Miller," Emma answered, choking back her tears. "A letter like that ought to be good for an extra three or four years of therapy."

"Emma?" Carrie said quietly.

"Yes?"

"Don't take this the wrong way," Carrie began slowly, "but . . . well, I think Kurt has a right to be mad, the same way you had a right to do what you did."

Emma nodded. "That's true," she replied, "but that doesn't make it hurt any less to hear it."

"So what about my fine brother?" Sam asked.

Emma reached into her pocketbook again and took out another letter. This one she handed to Sam.

"I get the honors?" Sam asked.

"He's in your family," Emma answered. "Besides, he said that you should read it."

"What are you talking about?" Carrie asked, puzzled.

"Just listen," Emma answered. "It's pure Adam."

Sam took the letter out of the envelope, unfolded it, and scanned it. Then she began to read aloud:

Dear Emma,

Sam called me right after we were all in New York, and she asked me not to contact you for a while, and I can't say I blame her. But I couldn't stop myself. So, if you're going to talk with her and Carrie about getting this letter—which you probably will, then at least give me the pleasure of knowing that Sam is the one who reads it out loud to the three of you!

A sense of humor above everything, that's my motto.

When I saw you in New York, it was wonderful, and I found out all over again how really special you are. I know you're confused, and I know I have something to do with that. I'm sorry about that, but I'm not sorry that you came with me that day instead of marrying him. You did the right thing, and no one can take doing the right thing away from you.

I will always be there for you when you are ready for me. I just hope it's soon. Actually, even sooner than that.

Okay Sam, stop making faces. I'm talking from the heart.

Love,
Adam

"Whoa, baby" was all Sam could comment. "I can't fault his taste," Carrie said with a small smile.

"I gotta hand it to you, Emma," Sam said quickly, "you are today's champ in the male attention department."

"I wish I wasn't," Emma sighed.

"Hey, just 'cause they're paying attention to you doesn't mean you have to pay attention back," Sam pointed out.

"I know that."

"So," Carrie asked, "what do you think?"

"I'll tell you what she thinks," Sam replied quickly. "She thinks Adam is the coolest but doesn't want anything to do with him now, and she thinks Kurt isn't right for her and she did the right thing, but she still loves him and she feels really, really guilty about what happened." Sam turned to Emma. "Am I right or am I right?"

Emma grinned at her. "Maybe I should make my appointment with you, and not with Mrs. Miller."

"I'm a lot cheaper," Sam admitted.

"Less expensive," Carrie corrected. "Diana is cheap, you're less expensive."

"Good distinction," Sam agreed. She lay back down on her beach mat. "Anyway, after this thing with the Flirts tonight, I may be heading for the old therapist's couch, too."

Emma covered her face with her hands. "I can't believe I have to face that tonight, on top of everything else."

"Well, you don't *have* to," Carrie pointed out. "The guys just said they'd like it if we would come."

186

Sam sighed. "I don't know what would be worse—being there or not being there."

"Me, either," Emma agreed sadly.

Word of the Flirts' "surprise" show at the Play Café had spread like wildfire around the island, so when Emma, Sam, and Carrie showed up at the club at ten o'clock, the place was packed.

Fortunately, Pres and Billy had reserved a table for them—their usual spot under the video monitor—and had marked it with a placard that read RESERVED: MISS CRESSWELL, MISS BRIDGES, MISS ALDEN, and had even arranged for drinks and snacks to be waiting for them.

"Kind of like a wake," Sam commented on seeing the spread. "Only the food is worse. At least we look incredible."

"Feel your worst, look your best," Emma quipped as they sat down, "isn't that your motto?"

"Well, it works, doesn't it?" Sam asked. She had on a black lace babydoll top over an antique black camisole, black tights and her red cowboy boots. Carrie had on a long flowery summer dress that unbuttoned from the bottom to show off a white lace slip, and combat boots on her feet. And Emma—in a real fashion departure from her usual look— had on worn jeans, a white T-shirt, and Sam's black leather jacket with Minnie Mouse painted on the back. They were nervous and had all made an extra effort. They were not about to let Diana and her backup singers show them up.

"Do you get the distinct impression everyone is looking at us?" Sam asked, noticing the people in the cafe pointing and whispering.

"How can you say that?" Carrie joked. "Just because everyone is turned this way, craning their necks with their eyes popping out."

"I don't know who these people are that keep taking our pictures," Sam said, a fake smile for the cameras plastered on her face.

"From newspapers, I guess," Carrie said. "The Flirts are news now that they got a big deal."

"Any publicity is good publicity," Sam maintained once again. "But I kind of hate this."

"Me, too," Emma agreed, sounding miserable.

"Hey, I say we look totally confident, like we're having the time of our lives," Sam decreed. "I absolutely will not let Diana De Witt see that I am upset. Are you guys with me on this?"

"We're with you," Carrie agreed. "Em?"

Emma nodded firmly.

"Cool," Sam said. "Now, let's see how nervous we can make Diana."

Sam looked up at the small Play Café stage, where a couple of tech-types were fiddling around with the sound system and mikes. One of them nodded to the other, and then the two of them left the stage.

Then, the entire cafe went dark, and the two hundred or so people inside, including about fifty who were packed in front of the stage on the small dance floor, erupted in applause. Everyone knew about the pending Polimar Records deal, and everyone was cheering for the hometown band.

I should be up there hearing that, Sam thought miserably. She gulped hard and willed herself not to cry. *I can't believe I'm not in the band anymore. I feel like my heart is breaking.*

The band had run into their places during

the blackout. Suddenly, a barrage of spotlights hit the stage. When the lights hit them, they charged into a tune Pres had written, called "Maybe."

Maybe we're together
Maybe we're apart.
Maybe I can't see what's in your heart.
Maybe you've got feelings
Or maybe you're too tough.
But if you want to take a chance, maybe it's love. . . .

Pres had the lead vocal, and while he was singing the last line of the first verse, he snuck a glance directly at Sam. Sam wasn't paying any attention, however. Her eyes were directly on Kimber, Maia, and Diana.

Even though they had rehearsed together, Maia still missed the high harmony line right off the bat, Sam noticed with satisfaction. *And Kimber blew the first dance combination.*

Sam's attention, and Emma's and Carrie's too, was focused directly on the backup singers throughout the entire song. When it was over, the girls turned to each other.

"Fair" was Emma's only comment. But there was pure ice in her eyes.

"They sucked," Sam responded. "We are so much better and the guys know it. Diana, too." She stared directly at Diana, but Diana was looking in every direction but Sam's.

The crowd quieted, and Billy started to speak.

"We're only doing one more tune," he said. "This one is for three of our very best friends. I think you all know who I'm talking about."

Huh, Sam thought. *They were going to do three tunes. I guess the girls could only learn two this quickly. And the dedication is nice. But, oh God, I'd rather be up there!*

The band launched into one of their newest uptempo numbers, called "On and Forever." And Sam could see that the two new backups were having the same trouble as they did on the first tune. The song ended to thunderous applause, though, and when the Flirts left the stage, there was so much chanting for an encore that the band came back out.

Pres quieted the crowd. Then, he went back to Sly in the drummer's position, reached down, and picked up his acoustic guitar. The crowd looked on, puzzled.

"What's he doing?" Emma whispered.

"Beats me," Sam responded. "But I'd bet anything those girls didn't learn a third number yet."

When the Play Café was so quiet Sam thought she could hear the sound of foghorns off in the distance, Pres began to fingerpick on the guitar. And then he alone began to sing the words to an old spiritual. It was a song the three girls knew very, very well:

Sometimes I feel like a motherless child
Sometimes I feel like a motherless child
Sometimes I feel like a motherless child
Such a long, long, long, long way from home . . .

The song was Pres's to sing. The three backups just stood there, like empty bottles floating on a pond. In fact, none of the other Flirts sang at all, until the very last line, when Billy, Jay, and Sly all came in on a perfect, four-part harmony.

Such a long, long, long, long, long way from home.

The crowd cheered, and Sam, Emma, and Carrie found themselves cheering, too. Even though she felt like crying Sam had to smile, because this very song was the song Emma had sung when she first auditioned to be in the Flirts. *It was also the song I sang when I reauditioned for the Flirts after dropping out and realizing what a stupid mistake it was,* Sam thought. She looked over at Emma, who had tears in her eyes.

"We'll make it through this," Sam vowed to Emma over the cheering crowd.

"No one misses us at all," Emma called back.

No one in the crowd was looking at them now; all eyes were focused on the stage.

It really was over.

"I thought you were meeting Pres afterward," Carrie said to Sam quietly as she drove Emma and Sam back to the Hewitts' and the Jacobses', respectively.

"I am," Sam replied, "he's picking me up later."

Carrie shrugged, and continued driving. Everyone was too depressed to talk.

"Mind if I turn on the radio?" Carrie asked. No one said a word. Carrie clicked it on. The tail end of the news blared out, the newscaster giving a report on the latest doings in the state house of representatives.

"Change the station," Sam ordered.

"Just a sec," Carrie said, "the news is just about over."

Then there was a commercial, and then the news came back on.

In the world of business today, the Dow Jones Industrial Average lost 16 points. Meanwhile, the entertainment world is buzzing as De Witt Enterprises, Inc., which recently purchased Polimar Records, reportedly sold Polimar tonight to a Japanese conglomerate that also has significant broadcast and other media holdings . . .

"Oh, my God," Sam cried, "did you guys hear that?"

"I think I did," Emma said, "but maybe I just wished it."

Carrie gave her friends a huge grin. "I

heard it. I definitely heard it. Diana's father sold Polimar!"

As if on cue, all three girls screamed together with happiness.

THIRTEEN

"A band meeting!" Sam yelled the next morning as she drove toward the Flirts' house. "We're going to a band meeting!" She looked over at Emma, who sat next to her, and she could feel Carrie grinning from the backseat.

When she'd gotten home the night before, Pres had called almost immediately with the news that Diana's dad had sold Polimar. Evidently Diana already knew, which was why she wouldn't even look at Sam during the gig. She hadn't told the band until afterward, and then—according to Pres—she tried to make a case that the band was better now and how they should continue in the same direction.

The guys in the band hadn't bought into

that for one second. They'd held a quick meeting and voted unanimously to bring Sam and Emma back and let Maia and Kimber go. As for Diana, her fate would be decided at today's band meeting.

"I can't wait to see her face," Sam exclaimed joyously. "This is one of the happiest days of my life!"

"Do you think Kimber and Maia took it okay?" Carrie asked.

"Oh, stop being so nice," Sam chided. "They were in the band for like two seconds." Sam hugged herself with one hand and steered the car with the other. "I could burst from happiness!"

Sam pulled the car into the Flirts' driveway—she noticed that Diana's jade-green Porsche had already arrived.

"I never thought I would look forward to seeing Diana De Witt," Sam said giddily as she got out of the car. "Ha!"

"Just try not to gloat too much," Carrie counseled.

"Wrong-amundo!" Sam declared. "I am going to love every moment of this."

When Sam knocked, Sly opened the door, and he did an uncharacteristic thing—he enveloped Sam, then Emma, then Carrie in a huge hug.

"I'm so glad to see you guys," he said, his eyes shining.

"Right back atcha," Sam replied, punching him lightly in the arm.

"No hard feelings about . . . you know?" Sly asked Sam.

"Hey, it's over," Sam said. "Anyway, I understood how you felt."

Sly smiled. "I underestimated you, Sam," he said.

Sam wriggled her eyebrows at him playfully. "A dangerous thing to do," she decreed, striding into the living room. Everyone was there. Diana was sitting in a faded overstuffed chair, her hands demurely folded in her lap.

"Hi, Diana!" Sam called to her with a little wave. "Long time, no see!" Diana tossed her curls and looked away.

Pres stifled a chuckle and came over to hug Sam. "I'm happy to see you, lady," he said in a low voice. "I'm sorry we didn't get together last night, but we had to make some big decisions about the band."

"It's cool," Sam replied.

He hugged her again. "We'll talk later."

Billy called the meeting to order. "This band has gone through a lot of changes lately," he said to the roomful of people. "As you all know by now, Clinton De Witt sold Polimar yesterday."

"So, do we still have a contract with them?" Jay wanted to know.

"I called our lawyer this morning to ask him about that," Billy said. "He has to check on a few things, but basically a deal is a deal. Now, they can buy us out if they want to— meaning we'd get some small bucks and they wouldn't proceed with our record—but we'll just have to wait and see."

"My father happens to be very close to the new head of the label," Diana said. "So don't think he doesn't have any influence anymore."

"Really?" Billy asked. "That's strange, because when I called Shelly Plotkin this morning, he told me your dad doesn't even know Karo Hashimuki—he's our new boss."

"Well, Shelly is wrong," Diana maintained.

"When did he meet him?" Billy asked innocently.

"They . . . they sat down recently and

talked all of this over," Diana said, folding her arms defensively. "And this new guy plans to follow exactly what my dad started." She gave Sam a mean look. "Which means you guys will be in major trouble when he finds out you axed Kimber and Maia."

Billy smiled. "I'm trying to figure out how your dad had a meeting with Mr. Hashimuki when Mr. Hashimuki was in a monastery in Tibet."

Diana's face paled. "Who told you that?"

"There's a big article about him in this morning's *Wall Street Journal*," Billy explained. "I read it."

Diana's eyes narrowed. "Don't make me laugh. You don't read the *Wall Street Journal*."

Billy grinned. "I do when my lawyer calls me and tells me to read it."

"Busted!" Sam cried gleefully.

Diana made a low noise under her breath, but she didn't say a word.

"I gotta say, I like the way this room looks," Pres said in his easy drawl. He nodded with satisfaction at Emma and Sam, then his eyes lit on Diana. "Hmmm, maybe not."

"What?" Diana asked.

"Maybe we still have a problem," Pres said slowly.

Diana crossed her legs nervously. "Look, I'm willing to work with Sam and Emma again, if that's what you're getting at."

Pres cocked his head to one side. "I think the question might be, are they willing to work with *you*?"

Sam had to bite her lip from laughing out loud. She stole a look at Emma, who had a huge grin on her face.

"What we need to do here is to take a vote," Billy said, "on whether Diana gets to stay in the band."

Diana's eyes narrowed dangerously. "You're kidding."

"Oh, I never kid about the band," Billy assured her.

"But you need me!" Diana protested. "I look good, I sound good, I move great—"

"Such a modest little thing," Sam said cheerfully. "I've always admired that about you."

Sam could tell that Diana was dying to tell her off, but she struggled to sound civil. "What's past is past, don't you think?" she asked everyone, her eyes searching the room.

"I mean, we've worked really hard—why go back to square one?"

"You were certainly willing to do that when you decided to kick us out of the band," Emma reminded her.

"That wasn't me, that was my father!" Diana protested.

"Gee, Shelly told me your father never actually even heard our demo tape," Billy told Diana. "Shelly said that your father said you could have anything you wanted, as long as it didn't cost him any extra money—that's a quote."

"Well . . . well . . . maybe Shelly is wrong," Diana tried, sounding feeble.

Billy shot her a look that said "get real."

"Okay, are we ready to vote on Diana?" he asked the group.

"Backups don't vote," Diana reminded Billy quickly, clearly grasping at straws.

"They do on this," Billy told her. "Let me see a show of hands for those that think Diana De Witt should be out of the Flirts as of right this minute."

Every hand in the room shot into the air.

Billy turned to Diana. "Gee, it's unanimous."

Diana jumped up. "I don't have to take this crap from you lowlifes! I really don't!"

"Bye-bye, Diana," Sam said, waving at the irate girl.

Diana picked up her purse and swung the shoulder strap over her shoulder. "You'll be sorry," she ranted. "You haven't heard the last about this, I'm warning you." Then she stomped out the front door, slamming it behind her.

There was a silence in the room, then finally Sam jumped up. "Hoorah! The Wicked Witch is dead!" Then she started dancing around the living room like a crazy person, singing "Ding-Dong, the Witch Is Dead" from *The Wizard of Oz*. Everyone in the band fell over laughing.

"I have to tell you," Sam said, falling breathlessly back into her chair, "that was truly one of the great moments of my life."

"We probably should have gotten rid of her a long time ago," Jay Bailey said. "She's trouble."

"And now she's someone else's trouble!" Sly added happily. He looked at Billy for reassurance. "We do still have a deal, right?"

"According to Shelly," Billy said. "Remember, he was interested in us way before this whole thing with De Witt."

"That's true," Sly agreed.

Billy looked over at Carrie. "I think Ian is gonna be pretty bummed, though. Shelly says Polimar wants to wait a little while—to let the Zits sound 'mature.' They're dropping that whole deal immediately. It turns out it was all Diana's idea. And Shelly was really only interested in getting on Graham's good side. Which, I might add, didn't work."

"Poor Ian." Carrie sighed.

"I knew it was her idea, I just knew it!" Sam exclaimed.

Pres disappeared into the kitchen and came back with a bottle of sparkling cider. "Somehow we just knew how this vote was gonna go down, and we prepared to celebrate." He popped the cork and everyone cheered. Sly handed out glasses all around, and Pres poured the bubbly.

"To the Flirts, back the way we're supposed to be," Pres said, holding up his glass.

"The Flirts!" everyone repeated, and then they all sipped from their glasses.

Jay slipped their demo tape into the cassette player, and the sounds of "Love Junkie" filled the air.

"It looks like we're gonna have to let Kimber go," Billy said. "Maia was our first choice. I guess she'll be Diana's replacement now!"

"Next time we do a road trip—hopefully to promote our CD—it'll be almost the same old gang, minus Diana—hoorah," Jay said.

Sam saw Emma flinch. She walked over to her friend.

"You okay?"

Emma nodded. "It's just what Jay said—'same old gang.' Kurt was the road manager on that trip. . . ."

Sam took a sip of her sparkling cider. "You'll get over him, Em. It takes time."

Emma sighed. "Well, the Peace Corps won't take me until I have at least another year of college, I'm too mixed up to get involved with Adam—or anyone else, for that matter—so I guess I'll have plenty of time on my hands."

"Hey, at least you're back in the band," Sam pointed out.

Emma grinned. "That means a lot."

Carrie came over to them. "It's great, huh? No more Diana. You two must be so happy."

"Emma's still moping over you-know-who," Sam said.

Carrie hugged Emma. "It's okay, Em. Just because you're the one who did the leaving doesn't mean that your heart isn't broken."

Emma smiled at Carrie. "Thanks," she said quietly. She looked at Sam. "To both of you. You guys really are a big help."

"Yeah, we are kind of fab-u-lous," Sam agreed downing the last of her sparkling cider. "Yum, this stuff is delicious."

"Want more?" Pres asked, coming up behind her with another bottle.

"Nah," Sam said. "I have to go back to work. Although as far as I'm concerned, the day that Diana De Witt is out of my life should be a national holiday!"

"Could I talk to you in the kitchen a sec?" Pres asked Sam.

"Lead the way," Sam said, taking Pres's hand.

They walked into the kitchen and Pres turned to her.

"Well, as my Jewish relatives would say, '*nu*?'" Sam asked. "That translates as 'What's up?'"

Pres put his arms around Sam's waist.

"Hey, did I mention how fine you looked last night in that black lacy thing you were wearin'?" Pres asked.

Sam smiled. "Gee, you noticed."

"I noticed."

"Glad to see I haven't lost my touch," Sam said lightly.

Pres stroked her hair. "It's more than that, Sam," he said in a low voice. "You've changed on the inside—your outside has always been hot stuff, and you know it."

"That's true," Sam agreed.

Pres swatted her butt playfully. "You know what I'm sayin' here."

Sam forced herself to be serious. "I think I do."

"I'm not saying we can jump right back into a big ol' commitment thing," Pres continued. "But . . . I want you back in my life, assuming you still want me back. Do you?" he asked.

"I do," Sam said quietly.

"I do," Pres confirmed. "I believe things'll be different this time, don't you?"

"Yeah," Sam agreed. She bit her lower lip. "I . . . I still get scared, you know? I'm afraid I'll mess this up."

"You won't," Pres told her.

"I don't know why you have so much faith in me," Sam replied.

"'Cuz I'm real smart," Pres whispered, and then he leaned over and softly kissed her lips.

"This doesn't mean we have to, like, jump into bed, right?" Sam asked nervously.

Pres threw his head back and laughed. "No, I thought we'd just do it right here on the kitchen counter." Sam looked panicked. "I'm kidding, Sam," Pres said. "I'm not tryin' to rush you into bed, okay?"

"Okay," Sam agreed with relief. "Because to tell you the truth . . . that's something else that scares me."

"It's okay," Pres assured her. "We've got all the time in the world."

Sam grinned happily. "We do, don't we?" She lifted her face and kissed Pres. "Wow, I got rid of Diana and I got you back, all in the same day. It's almost too much happiness for a girl to take!"

"Almost, but not quite," Pres teased.

Then he pulled her to him and kissed her until she felt breathless.

"Does this mean that you, uh, like me a lot?" Sam asked.

"It means I love you," Pres replied, a lazy grin playing around his lips.

Sam felt a thrill of happiness from the bottoms of her feet to the ends of the hair on her head. "Right back atcha," she told him.

"Unh-uh," Pres said. "You have to say it. No jokes. Just put yourself right out there on the line, girl."

Pres stared her in the eye. Sam stared back. She gulped hard. *It's now or never,* she told herself. *Take the plunge. He isn't going to hurt you. I hope. Anyhow, you have to take the risk.* "I love you, too," she finally said. "I really, really love you."

And she meant it with all her heart.

SUNSET ISLAND MAILBOX

Dear Readers,

First of all, I have to tell you that I've been working on the most exciting thing for all of you: the first Sunset Island product. Oh, I wish I could tell you more, but I don't want to spoil the surprise! Okay, I can say this . . . you'll know exactly what it is in July, and I'm hoping that you'll love it as much as I do. Look for more developments in the next book!

Oh, listen to this—I've got a great story for you. Recently, I was opening my fan mail (my favorite thing to do) and I found a letter from . . . a guy! And he sent photos! His name is Jeremy Thompson and he's a cute seventeen-year-old high-school senior. He's a real Kurt Ackerman type, if you ask me. He was introduced to the island by his friend Staci. So . . . I picked up the phone and I called him! We had a great conversation, and I found out he's a real die-hard Sunset Island fan. And then I came up with an idea: to let all of you become his pen pals. He is totally thrilled with the idea, and promises to answer your letters. This is how to get a letter to Jeremy:

Cherie Bennett
For: Jeremy Thompson
c/o General Licensing Company
24 West 25th Street
New York, New York 10010

I will forward your letters. And of course I promise that no one but Jeremy will open or read his mail.

I recently had lunch dates with two wonderful readers. Jeff and I met with Leah Peterzell and her dad in Nashville. Leah lives in Knoxville and she's a basketball star at her school. Then, over Thanksgiving vacation, we were in North Carolina visiting my mom, and we had lunch with Stephanie Staton and her mother. Stephanie is such a cutie! She's also a future actress and writer.

Anyway, keep those cards, letters, and photos coming, folks! You guys are the greatest, coolest, most wonderful readers in the world!

See you on the island!
Best-
Cherie Bennett

Cherie Bennett
c/o General Licensing Company, Inc.
24 West 25th Street
New York, New York 10010

Hi Cherie,

My name is Anee. I'm thirteen, and I love your books. My friends and I share them all. I just finished reading Sunset Touch *and I really learned a lot about friendship from it. I learned from Sam's mistakes that sometimes you have to take risks if you want a friendship to last. I think that after reading this book I will be more sensitive to other people's feelings, because now I know better. And the funny thing is, I don't think that you even meant for the book to come through that way. By the way, did you base Sam and Susan on yourself?*

> *Your friend,*
> *Anee Miltich*
> *Fergus Falls, Minnesota*

Dear Anee,

I really loved your letter. It's important to be sensitive to others—okay that's a real "duh." But what I mean is that it was important for Sam to be both understanding and accepting of who X really is. I didn't base Susan on myself at all; I just made her up. But as I've always said, Sam is the character I relate to the most, especially when she's cracking jokes.

> Best,
> Cherie

Dear Cherie,

I am a sixteen-year-old student at Savannah High School and I love all of your books. They are the only books I read besides school books. Reading helps with everything and now I actually enjoy doing it. If your books hadn't been published I wouldn't know what to do about a lot of my problems. You got me interested in reading and I will always love you for it. What are your favorite books?

Sincerely,
Jennifer Burn
Pooler, Georgia

Dear Jennifer,

You absolutely made my day when you told me that you enjoy reading now. When I was a teenager I loved to read, but I hear from a lot of kids who tell me they don't. Believe me, reading is the key to so much in life. Some of my favorite novels are: <u>To Kill a Mockingbird</u> by Harper Lee, <u>The Heart Is a Lonely Hunter</u> by Carson McCullers, <u>The Chosen</u> by Chaim Potok, and <u>Exodus</u> by Leon Uris. What are your favorite novels out there?

Best,
Cherie

Dear Cherie,
Let me start by saying that I absolutely love your
Sunset Island books. They're extremely well writ-
ten and enjoyable to read. That is why I regret to
say that I was deeply offended when you degraded
baton twirling in your book Sunset After Dark. *I*
have been twirling for seven years. Like every
other baton twirler I know, I've practiced very
hard to achieve what I've won. I have earned
twelve Florida state titles, five regional, and two
world/national titles. Hard work, sweat, and
tears have brought me to where I am today. Not to
mention hours of strenuous practice. Thank you
for taking the time to read my letter.

Sincerely,
Susan E. Young
Pembroke, Florida

Dear Susan,

Congratulations on all your incredible suc-
cesses. I'm sure you've worked extremely
hard and I applaud you for it. It was not my
intention to denigrate baton twirling. You
must realize that because a character in a
novel—which is a work of fiction—feels a certain way, that does not mean that the author
feels the same. I definitely do not agree with
all the opinions and actions of my characters!
Still, you certainly make a valid point about
how easy it can be to deprecate certain sports
that we think of as "female," like baton twirling and cheerleading. I mean, what is so in-

trinsically superior about succeeding at, say, football or baseball? I say more power to you! You have every right to feel proud of your accomplishments!

Best,
Cherie

SUNSET ISLAND ™

Sam, Carrie, and Emma return to Sunset Island and their summer jobs as au pairs...Let the adventure begin!

By Cherie Bennett

__SUNSET HEAT   0-425-13383-4/$3.99

Sam is hired by a talent scout to dance in a show in Japan. Unfortunately, Emma and Carrie don't share her enthusiasm. No one really knows if this is on the up and up, especially after her fiasco with the shifty photographer last summer. But Sam is determined to go despite her friends. . .

__SUNSET PROMISES   0-425-13384-2/$3.99

Carrie receives a lot of attention when she shows her photos at the Sunset Gallery. She is approached by a publisher who wants her to do a book of pictures of the island. But when Carrie photographs the entire island, she discovers a part of Sunset Island that tourists never see...

__SUNSET SCANDAL   0-425-13385-0/$3.99

Emma has started to see Kurt again, and everything's going great...until Kurt is arrested as the suspect in a rash of robberies! He has no alibi, and things look pretty bad. Then, Emma befriends a new girl on the island who might be able to help prove Kurt's innocence.

__SUNSET WHISPERS   0-425-13386-9/$3.99

Sam is shocked to find out she is adopted. She's never needed her friends more than when her birth mother comes to Sunset Island to meet her. And to add to the chaos, Sam and Emma, along with the rest of the girls on the island, are auditioning to be backup in the rock band Flirting With Danger.
